## ...ES' TRAIL

Forbes is a drifter who doesn't want responsibilities. However, things change when he meets Ira Hamilton, foreman of a ranch owned by Richard Wallace. Getting on Hamilton's wrong side, Forbes is forced to accept a job on the ranch—and he soon realises that all is not as it seems. When he falls in love with a young widow who is being threatened by Wallace, he decides it's time to make a stand.

# FORBES' TRAIL

# FORBES' TRAIL

*by*

Steven Gray

**Dales Large Print Books**
Long Preston, North Yorkshire,
England.

British Library Cataloguing in Publication Data.

Gray, Steven
    Forbes' trail.

A catalogue record for this book is
available from the British Library

ISBN 1-85389-599-7 pbk

First published in Great Britain by Robert Hale Ltd., 1994

Published in Large Print January, 1996 by arrangement with
Robert Hale Ltd.

Dales Large Print is an imprint of
Library Magna Books Ltd.
Printed and bound in Great Britain by
T.J. Press (Padstow) Ltd., Cornwall, PL28 8RW.

# ONE

Forbes stared in the scrap of mirror he kept for shaving. Looking back at him were bleary brown eyes, a whiskered chin and black hair hanging in tangles almost to his shoulders.

'Oh God,' he groaned out loud. 'I'm getting much too old for this sort of life.'

It wasn't fun any more, waking up on the freezing hard ground, his body suffering various aches and pains. What he needed was a nice soft bed and a nice soft woman to share it with. But for certain no woman would want to share what he had here.

He'd made camp the night before in a spot by a fast running creek, where the winter snow had disappeared. The camp was sparse and, like Forbes himself, untidy. Merely a fire, now a bank of cold ashes, surrounded by his few possessions: scrawny horse, saddle, two threadbare blankets, the down at heel boots, jeans, plaid shirt and frayed coat. An old dirty slicker provided extra warmth during the day and a groundsheet at night.

Scraping away at his dark whiskers, and suffering a fit of despair, Forbes came to his usual conclusion.

He'd reform—tomorrow. Today, town still beckoned.

Not that "town" was perhaps the right word for the ramshackle collection of buildings into which Forbes rode later on that afternoon. It was so small it didn't even have a name. But it wasn't the quantity of the buildings which concerned Forbes, only the quality, and who would complain about that?

After all what could be better than a couple of saloons, where the drink was cheap and powerful, and a cathouse, where the girls performed in much the same manner?

The general store and the boarding house he dismissed. If an evening of poker went well he might be able to afford something from the store but it was doubtful he'd ever sleep in the boarding house. With enough money he'd spend the night in the arms of a whore. Otherwise it would be the livery stable.

The town had no decent women and hardly any decent men. But there weren't any hard-assed desperadoes either. And while most of the girls weren't exactly in their first bloom of youth and enthusiasm, neither were they yet raddled and haggard.

It was the sort of place Forbes felt at home in; full of no-hopers on the slide but still not quite at rock bottom. Just like him. It was good to be among familiar, friendly faces.

'Forbes!' The squeal of delight came from the brothel's verandah.

He looked up and grinned as a half-breed girl of immense proportions waved to him, setting her ample flesh wobbling. Sallee was half French, half Pawnee and wholly wild. He decided to make the cathouse his first stop.

'What is matter?' Sallee asked in her

broken and atrociously accented English. 'You un'appy?'

Forbes rolled away from her, sat up in the bed and reached over to make himself a cigarette. He hadn't realized his mood had affected his performance but Sallee was experienced in the ways of men.

'Sallee, I'm thirty-five and what do I have to show for it?'

'You 'ave me.'

'Cathouses, gambling and drinking were all very fine when I was young. But I ain't young any more. It's leading me nowhere. I ain't even a successful enough thief to have a price on my head!'

Sallee stroked his arm. 'Time to settle down, mebbe.'

'How? I ain't ever managed to save any money and I ain't got any skills.'

'You tell me you know little of cattle.'

'Yeah and a little about farming, even a bit about clerking in a store. But who the hell wants to be a cowboy, farmer or a clerk? Not me honey.'

'You no want wife? Kids?'

'Hell, no thanks.' A family meant

10

ties and duties, things Forbes could do without.

'Then I make you 'appy.' Giggling Sallee grabbed at him, the blanket falling to the floor.

Quickly Forbes stubbed out his cigarette. Sallee didn't understand what he was talking about—but what the hell? She was here with him, now, in her warm bed, that was all that mattered. Things were looking up all the time. His earlier desolate mood vanished in the thoughts of whiskey, women and cards. He might be getting old but by God he wasn't ancient; he had a few good years left in him yet. Time to think of reforming when they'd gone by.

Earlier Forbes had stabled his horse at the livery; down by the cattle pens. The pens had been built some years before by the hopeful citizens who'd believed that the railroad was going to run a spur line to their town and that the ranchers would bring their cattle here for shipping to market. In the event, the railroad had never come anywhere near and the only reason for any cattlemen's rare presence was to drink and whore. Usually the pens lay empty and rotting. That afternoon Forbes had been surprised to see forty or so head of prime beeves corralled in the first pen, bawling and kicking about in the mud as cattle usually did.

After leaving Sallee, who had a living to earn and couldn't spend all her time with someone with no money, Forbes naturally gravitated to the nearest saloon. In the smoky atmosphere, among the battered pieces of furniture and the sawdust on the floor, Ben Cook, bartender and mixer of evil brews, greeted him like an old friend; which was natural because when Forbes was in town he drank more than anyone else.

'Yeah, that's right, cattle,' Cook said, pouring out, without being asked, a glass of Forbes' favourite brand of snakejuice.

'Where do they come from?'

'Belong to some fancy gent from back East, who's passing through, having set up a ranch over Fairmont way. Staying in the boarding house and it didn't look like it suited him much. Travelling on tomorrow. He's with his foreman. That's the gent over there in the corner.'

Curiously Forbes looked across at the stranger.

He was in his late thirties, with dark hair, balding in the front, and a small scar on his upper lip. His posture was one of idleness but there was nothing idle about his hard eyes as he surveyed the room.

'Not my type.' Forbes turned back to Cook and changed the subject. 'Much happening around here?'

'Oh, you know, rumours about this or that.' There always were rumours which so far had never amounted to anything. 'What about you? Last we heard you was over in Montana.'

'Yeah,' Forbes admitted. 'The least said about Montana the better.' Montana was an incident he preferred to forget.

A couple of youngsters had persuaded him to rob a country store. Nothing to it, they'd said in their wide-eyed, excited way. And like a fool, he'd agreed. Nothing to it all right, except a clerk who'd raised the alarm and a posse of concerned citizens in pursuit. That was the closest he'd ever come to being arrested, or even shot at.

Then his companions had stolen from him the little they'd stolen from the store. Deciding discretion was better than getting even, Forbes skedaddled back to Wyoming, where he felt safe amongst people he knew.

The experience had saddened him. You couldn't trust anyone these days. And made him realize it was better to stick to what you knew, with who you knew.

'Let's just say I should have stayed in town during the winter doing odd jobs, not gone chasing off after easy money and ending up freezing my butt off in the hills.'

'True,' said Cook, not saying anything about it being doubtful whether Forbes would ever learn sense.

The two men stayed at the bar, talking over old times. Or rather Forbes listened to what Cook, who, having once been a mountain man had a fund of untrue tall tales, had to say. And drinking.

After several glasses life began to look as good as ever. He must be the fool everyone considered him to even think of changing, of settling down. Look at what he had now! Money enough to buy drinks, good friends, Sallee waiting for him. No one to tell him what to do, or when to do it, no obligations.

And the chance to gamble.

For as the evening wore on, so more people came into the saloon. Some were those who lived in and made a precarious living from the town, others were cowboys from nearby ranches. They all wanted the same thing as Forbes: a good time. And for some that meant sitting round a table playing poker.

Soon a game started up and soon Forbes wandered over to join it.

Naturally Forbes cheated. Not too much but just enough so that while he didn't exactly win a fortune, neither would he come out a loser.

It wasn't as if he was the only one. Most everyone he played with did the same. It was accepted, even expected. Those who didn't cheat were idiots or greenhorns and deserved to be rooked.

But that night it was different. The rancher's hard eyed foreman joined in the game. And he didn't cheat. Neither was he an idiot nor a greenhorn.

Forbes felt the game was going well. Besides himself and the foreman, there were two very young cowboys, who were easy enough to fleece, and the boarding house owner, always an inept player. To make it look right, he'd lost the first couple of games, won the next one, lost a couple more and then steadily won. The amounts on the table weren't great: the only one present with anything in the way of money was the foreman; the other three were as broke as Forbes. The games weren't all that hard fought.

After a while, Forbes started to get anxious to finish up a winner and take himself back to Sallee's dusky, plump body. So perhaps his mind wasn't on what he was doing, perhaps for a moment he got careless.

'You cheating sonofabitch!'

The foreman's shout rang out across the saloon and all other noise abruptly stopped. As the other three poker players gaped at their two companions, everyone's attention came to rest on the table and more particularly on the foreman, who was red with fury, and on Forbes, who had come to a halt in reaching for the pot. Here was the chance of some excitement and no one was going to miss it.

'Hey, now, wait a minute!' Forbes made an attempt at disgruntled innocence.

'You goddamned cheat! That card,' the man reached over to tap one of the four kings with which Forbes thought he'd won the hand, 'was on the bottom of the deck last time out.'

'I shuffled the cards...'

'No, you never. I watched you most carefully, just like I been watching the last few hands you've played. You cheated at 'em all.'

Forbes had gone cold inside. What did he do now? To be called out as a cheat at cards, even if it was true, and not do anything about it, was to risk being called a coward.

Forbes wasn't a coward, even if he wasn't exactly brave either, and he didn't want to lose face in front of these people he called friends. He didn't want Sallee to hear that he'd sat shivering with fright and allowed himself to be insulted and bullied.

But to do anything about it meant going up against the hard eyed foreman. Forbes had a feeling he'd come out the loser in gun or fist fight. Maybe he wasn't a coward but he didn't like taking unnecessary risks either.

'You're making a mistake,' he said sulkily and, in the hope that the man would be prepared to let it go, added. 'Here, take the money, it ain't important.'

'I weren't mistaken.' Obviously the man wasn't going to let Forbes off that easily. 'I don't like cheats or being goddamned cheated!' His voice rose to a shout and suddenly his temper got the better of him. With a roar of anger he tipped up the table, scattering cards, money and glasses all over the floor, and scattering the poker players as well, as they scrambled out of the way.

Caught in the chest by the edge of the table, Forbes flew backwards. He landed with a thump, the table half on top of him. He managed to push the table out of the way, only to find the foreman standing over him, pointing a Colt 45 in his face and looking set to pull the trigger.

## TWO

Forbes was vaguely aware of Cook reaching under the bar for the shotgun he kept there. He wouldn't make it in time to save Forbes from being shot.

'Hold it right there, Ira!' The clipped Eastern tones rang imperiously round the saloon. 'It's not worth shooting a man over the measly amount of money you had in front of you.'

For a moment Forbes didn't think the

foreman was going to take any notice. Then slowly, reluctantly, a mutinous look on his face, he holstered his gun and stepped back. Forbes now saw that his rescuer was a young man in his late twenties, who looked completely out of place in the rough saloon. He was dressed in an expensive dark suit and highly polished boots, and was very good looking with slicked back reddish gold hair, blue eyes and a blond beard. Unlike everyone else, he wasn't carrying a weapon, or at least if he was it was expertly concealed, but held a gold topped cane in one hand and a derby hat in the other.

Forbes considered him a dandy but in the circumstances wasn't about to say so.

Forbes scrambled to his feet and, together with the other poker players, hefted the table and chairs upright. He then joined them in scrabbling around for the money scattered on the floor. It might not be very dignified but that money was all he had, he needed it. He wasn't some fancy, rich rancher from the East, who considered twenty bucks a measly amount of money. He'd been willing to give it up to save his skin but not otherwise.

When he stood up, the rancher, a bit of a sneer on his face, said, 'Come with me. Both of you. You look as if you could do with a drink. Bartender, look after my hat and cane.'

Before long the saloon was back to its normal, noisy self, the incident forgotten. As the three men huddled together in the corner by the bar, Forbes had to lean forward in order to hear all that the rancher was saying.

'My name's Richard Wallace. This is my foreman, Ira Hamilton.' Neither man offered to shake hands with a lowly specimen like Forbes. 'I daresay you realize I'm from the East.'

Forbes nodded.

'I'm out here to be a rancher. Last year my father purchased some land for me on my twenty-seventh birthday. It's over near the town of Fairmont. Do you know it?'

'Vaguely.'

Fairmont was about forty miles away at the head of a large valley leading towards the Rockies. Forbes had never actually visited the town but he'd passed close by on more than one occasion on his way to do this or that down in Colorado.

'Well, it's a nice area and I'm told the grass is good all year round. I'm determined to make the Rocking W into one of the largest and most successful ranches Wyoming, and indeed the whole of the West, has ever known. You see I'm a younger son and never destined to inherit anything from my father's banking business so I must make my own way in the world. You know what I mean?'

Forbes didn't know what the man was talking about but he thought another nod was in order.

'And I feel I must repay all that money my father has kindly spent on me and make him proud of me.'

This time Forbes didn't even bother to nod. He'd never had money spent on him, nor done anything to make anyone proud. He wasn't to know that if Wallace succeeded at ranching, it would be quite unlike all his other ventures that he'd started and that had ended in failure.

'Ambition is an honourable thing.'

Forbes had never had that either.

'Do you know much about ranching and cattle, Mr Forbes?'

'A bit.' Forbes' reply was guarded. He wasn't sure where this conversation was headed but he had an idea and he didn't like it much.

'I have a problem.'

Somehow that didn't come as any surprise.

'While most of my neighbours are law abiding hard workers, a number of them believe that as I'm from the East, I must be a greenhorn. They think they can rustle my cattle and get away with it.' Wallace downed his drink in indignation and signalled to Cook for a refill for them all.

Forbes said nothing. Wallace probably wouldn't appreciate the fact but in his younger days Forbes had ridden the rustling trail down in New Mexico and Arizona. That was where he'd learned about cattle. He hadn't been fond of the life or of the cows. The work had been hard and dangerous and the cows were awkward animals who thought they knew best.

'The local law, such as it is, doesn't seem willing or able to do anything to stop it. Everyone appears to be on the side of the homesteaders because they're poor. It doesn't matter that they're robbing me.'

Forbes felt uncomfortable. He didn't want any part of this. But he had a feeling he wasn't going to be offered a choice.

'I've hired Ira here not only as my foreman, a job at which he is very good, but also to help stop the rustlers.'

Looking at the foreman, Forbes just bet which part of the job he liked best.

'You're doing a good job, aren't you, Ira?'

'Yes, sir.' Hamilton spoke for the first time since Wallace had joined them.

'But he can't do it all on his own. He needs help. I want you to help him.'

Forbes was aware of Hamilton stiffening in surprise. Surely the man must have known where this conversation was leading.

'Hey, look now.' Forbes held up his hands in protest. 'I may be a bum and a cheat but I ain't into that sort of thing.'

A look of anger passed across Wallace's face. 'If by that sort of thing you mean acts of unnecessary violence, I can assure you I'm not into it either. I would never tolerate that.'

'I wouldn't have thought you'd be so particular,' Hamilton said to Forbes, making him bristle.

'Now, now,' Wallace put out a hand tapping his foreman's arm, 'there's no need for insults.' He took a sip of beer and fastidiously wiped his beard free of froth.

'How do you mean to stop the rustling if not by force?'

'I want guards put on my cattle and the rustlers identified and sentenced in a proper court of law. I'm not stupid, Mr Forbes, and I realize that out here in the West where everyone wears a gun sometimes people are going to get hurt. If one or two of them resist or start shooting at my men then they have only themselves to blame if my men shoot back. But I'm certainly not advocating gunning people down, with no provocation, whatever they may have done.'

Forbes wasn't sure he understood all that Wallace said. The man used a lot of big words he'd never heard before. But he understood the sentiments. If Wallace was telling the truth, he was being a lot more lenient than many ranchers would be towards rustlers, who if caught could usually expect only a rope dangling over a convenient tree.

'And if I refuse?'

Wallace smiled silkily. 'I believe I have you over a barrel, isn't that the phrase? You have one of two choices. You can either be handed over to Ira for the beating he believes you thoroughly deserve or you can accept the wage of sixty dollars a month, plus keep.'

Forbes blinked rapidly. Sixty dollars a month! That was more than he could ever beg, borrow, steal or especially earn in an ordinary job. This particular job might not be exactly what Wallace said, Forbes was convinced it had to involve some violence towards others, but he was able to justify that by thinking that rustlers were breaking the law and knew the risks they ran, and so put it out of his mind. For if the idea of a beating—and he was certain the foreman could and would give him one—didn't sway him, then the thought of all that money did.

'I'm in.'

'Good. We're leaving early in the morning. To be honest I can't wait to get out of this Godforsaken place. So be ready or I won't wait.'

'Yeah, sure, I'll be there.'

'And I don't want you suffering from a hangover. I believe in allowing my men to drink but not to get drunk.'

As that might not be so easy to accomplish, Forbes decided he'd better not stay in the saloon. He'd go back to the cathouse and celebrate his new found wealth and position with Sallee's charms. A bit unsteady on his feet he pushed his way through the crowd and disappeared into the night.

A scowl on his face, Hamilton watched him go. 'What did you hire him for?' he asked in a surly tone. 'He's nothing but a drunken bum. I bet he knows nothing about handling cattle.'

'Don't you think I know that? You and the others don't need help with the cattle, you can manage quite easily at the moment.'

Ira said nothing. This wasn't true, especially in the circumstances, but not only was Richard Wallace mean with his money and didn't want to pay anyone unnecessarily, preferring to spend it on things like looking good, more importantly, he didn't have much idea about running a ranch. And he didn't like accepting advice either, believing that he knew best.

'When the time comes I shall hire first class cowboys for the job. It shouldn't be difficult. They're already drifting into Fairmont looking to sign on for the summer. But, Ira, you do need help with those damned sodbusters. Someone like Forbes has brawn but very few brains and he's the kind will do anything for

28

money. And that's just what we want.'

'Yeah, I suppose so. But I don't like or trust him.'

'You don't have to. All you need do is keep an eye on him and make sure he does what he's told.'

'All right.'

Wallace smiled widely. 'Think of it this way. If anything goes wrong it'll be handy to have someone to blame, won't it?'

Slowly, Hamilton grinned back. 'Yeah, I guess it will at that.'

'Good morning, Mr Forbes,' Wallace said the next morning.

Dawn was only a streaking in the sky when Forbes, trying not to look as bleary-eyed as he felt after a night with Sallee, presented himself at the cattle pens.

Hamilton was already mounted and driving the cows into formation. 'Get a move on,' he said. 'We ain't got all day.'

Wallace, wearing a range outfit that must have cost the equivalent of half a year's wages for most cowboys, led out a beautiful thoroughbred mare and rode it to the front of the herd, which was where he stayed, doing no work, and keeping himself aloof from his two men, for the rest of the journey.

The drive across the swaying grasslands of Wyoming confirmed Forbes' opinion that cattle were awkward, dirty and dangerous animals, who did little but bawl incessantly and raise up a mess of dust.

And Hamilton was a bit the same. He made a lot of noise, shouting out his orders which usually resulted in Forbes bringing up the rear and getting covered in dust. He was extremely awkward and Forbes reckoned that when he liked, he could be dangerous. Though grudgingly admitting that he was a good cattleman, Forbes didn't like him.

Nor did he much like Richard Wallace. Of the little he saw of him, the rancher seemed an arrogant snob with more money than was good for him. But then maybe a lot of young men from wealthy Eastern families were the same.

While he wasn't much impressed by the rancher, he was surely impressed by the ranch.

The drive skirted Fairmont and followed the road running the length of the valley, most of which was Rocking W land. The entrance consisted of two pillars of wood with a beam of cows' horns twisted together between them at the top and the name of the ranch carved in wood hanging underneath. Beyond was prime land, foothills on three sides rising gently to the snow capped mountains. The cattle were let free to graze while the men continued on their ride to the ranch headquarters.

The house, a large stone building, had a porch running all the way round, steps leading up to an impressive front door, and glass in the windows. Smoke was coming out of a stone chimney in the roof. As Wallace dismounted in front of the house, a servant of some kind came running out to take his horse round to its separate stables.

Men, as well as animals, were also

separated: a bunkhouse for the ordinary cowboys and a one story shack for Hamilton. Beyond these were barns, corrals and various other storerooms and work buildings. All were in good repair.

Two young men came wandering up from the direction of the bunkhouse.

'Del, Burt,' Hamilton called to them. 'Meet Forbes. Our new hand. He'll be working mostly with me.'

'Pleased to meet you,' said Del. He was nice looking, with long fair hair, wispy blond moustache and blue eyes.

Burt was shorter and rather plump with dark curly hair and brown eyes. He said nothing but merely nodded in Forbes' direction.

'Show him where he can sleep, will you?'

'Yeah, come on Forbes.'

The bunkhouse had eight bunks in it, only two of which were occupied.

'Choose any one you like,' said Del.

Feeling he might want a bit of privacy, Forbes chose a bunk in the far corner well away from those where Del and Burt slept.

As he placed his few possessions in the chest that also served as a table, Del sat down on the bunk and said:

'You'll like it here. The work's not too bad, although there's plenty of it, and the food's good while we're round the ranchhouse 'cos Mr Wallace employs some foreign cook. Can't understand a damn word he says but his cooking's OK. 'Course it ain't so good out on the trail 'cos Burt gets to cook then. Me and Burt have been partners for years now.' Del nodded towards his friend who was dealing cards at the table in the middle of the room. 'He don't say much.'

Which was probably because the poor guy didn't get a chance with Del around doing all the talking, Forbes thought sourly.

'But he's OK. Ira is OK too once you get to know him.'

'I'm bushed,' Forbes said and sprawled on the bunk, arms behind his head, hoping Del would take the hint and shove off.

Del didn't. He continued talking for a while but eventually Forbes' grunted replies put him off. A bit huffily he went over to join Burt and they began to argue over the game of Patience Burt had been enjoying on his own.

## THREE

'You're sure you don't mind looking after Billy?'

'Of course I don't, Alice,' Mrs McGee smiled. She looked down at the small boy whose hand she firmly held. 'We're going to make some pastry and feed the chickens and collect the eggs, aren't we dear?'

Billy nodded.

'All right then, thanks.' Alice Munroe knew her son, shy, lonely and missing his father could be difficult when he liked. But Mrs McGee, a grandmother five times over, was used to children and wouldn't mind if he made a mess in her kitchen or chased the chickens a bit too enthusiastically. She could safely leave him with her. 'I shan't be long.' Shoving on her old hat, Alice left the boarding house.

It was a lovely early Spring morning: the sky a clear bright blue, the sun shining enough to warm the wind, the meadows surrounding the town already awash with colourful flowers. The mood she was in, it should have been raining.

The Deanes were going, leaving everything behind merely because Richard Wallace wanted them to. They were the third family to do so in the last month. Even now they were in town buying supplies for their journey to who knew where. Guy Deane had promised to stay and fight but clearly he'd been pressured into selling out by his wife who was scared for herself and her two sons. Alice couldn't really blame them but gradually her friends and neighbours were deserting the area and she feared that eventually she would be left to continue the fight all alone.

Hands clenched into fists, head lowered, Alice started across the road.

'Mind out!'

Startled she looked up and saw Ira

Hamilton and another man she didn't recognize, almost on the point of riding her down. Alice stepped quickly out of the way.

To her fury, Hamilton smiled and politely raised his hat. 'Morning ma'am. Out early I see.'

Alice scowled at him and said nothing, wishing she was a man and could start a fight with him, especially when he smiled mockingly.

'Who was that?' Forbes asked as they rode by her.

'Alice Munroe. She owns a place backing onto Mr Wallace's.'

'She didn't look as if she liked you much.'

Hamilton laughed. 'She doesn't.' He glanced back at Alice. 'Well, well, lookee there!'

Forbes turned in the saddle, following the man's gaze. A wagon stood by the general store, piled high with household goods. A woman sat on the wagon seat, two young boys beside her, while a man, who was loading up the supplies, had stopped to talk to Alice. They both glared back at Hamilton.

'Good.' Hamilton gave a self-satisfied smirk. 'That's the Deane family. Deane is one of the goddamned thieves we've had trouble with. He must have taken notice of Mr Wallace's warning and decided to leave.' He spat on the ground. 'One less rustler to worry about.'

Forbes had been at the ranch for a couple of days when that morning Hamilton said he needed to go into town to buy supplies. He wanted Forbes to go with him to show him what Fairmont was like. And he'd given him an advance on his salary so that he could buy some clothes and anything else he might need. Already bored with life out on the ranch with no one except Del and Burt for company, and hardly anything to drink, Forbes had been only too pleased about the trip, even if it did mean being with Ira.

Fairmont was a fair sized place, full of people and noise.

Riding along by the foreman, Forbes tried to take things in; or at least discover where the saloons and brothels were situated. They were all that interested him. The stores, the bank, the church—none of them meant anything. He'd been scared that a growing town, having found religion and education, might have done away with its sin, and he was pleased to see that the redlight district was still managing to thrive. Several saloons ranged from the expensive to the gaudily cheap, a couple of cathouses competed with small cribs. There was something for everyone.

Fairmont might be just a bit too busy and a bit too tame for Forbes' normal tastes, on the other hand it contained plenty of choice. He could probably have a good time here and find someone to have it with.

Alice's mood hadn't improved by lunch-time. It had, if anything got worse. There was only one person in town who she wanted to see and who could cheer her up. So she hurried along the sidewalk to the newspaper office where Casey Chapman would be getting ready to shut up and head for the cafe as he did every day at this time.

At her entrance, Chapman looked up from the printing press and smiled. 'Alice! I heard you were in town. I was hoping you'd come see me. What's the matter? You look angry.'

'Oh! And I thought I was hiding it so well.'

'I'm a newspaperman, my dear, I can always sense people's moods. That's how I get my stories.'

Alice laughed. 'I've spent the morning touring the saloons and the stores looking for someone to work for me. Everyone has been oh so polite, even in the Bull's Head...'

'You shouldn't have gone in there! Especially on your own. It'll soon be spread all round town by the gossips.'

Alice sighed. She knew very well that many of the townsfolk considered her not only strange but also wrong for not always acting in the way they thought she should. Her behaviour was often criticized both as unladylike, for how she dressed and spoke, and foolish, for staying on the ranch all on her own.

'Casey, I'm too desperate to act decently any more or care what other people say! Anyway I averted my eyes from the saloon's more dubious attractions.'

'What happened?'

'Can't you guess? Everyone declined my offer.' Alice's tone was bitter. 'I'm a woman and what does a woman know about running a ranch? I can't offer much in the way of wages. And there might be dangers. Why risk your life for a poverty stricken and ignorant woman? They're all laughing at me behind my back.'

'I'm sure that's not true.'

'Well they're all certainly waiting for me to quit.'

'Like the Deanes?'

'Exactly. I saw them earlier. I wish they weren't going but Mr Deane said they had to think of the children.'

'You've got a child. You're not leaving.'

Alice shrugged. 'I sometimes wonder why I don't. Oh, Casey, what annoys me so much is that it means Mr Richard

Wallace has got his greedy paws on yet another piece of land. Why can't he be content with what he's got already? It's a damn sight more than most of us have.'

'Some people are never content. Despite all the crap about being an impoverished younger son, Wallace has probably never been refused anything in his life before. So he can't understand why people should start refusing him now and it makes him more determined to have what he wants.' Chapman caught hold of Alice's hand for a moment. 'Be careful, Alice. Your land backs onto Wallace's and he has his eyes on it. He won't care that you want to keep it, any more than he cares that others want to keep the land they've owned and worked for years.'

'I know.'

'By the way Ira Hamilton is in town.'

'Yes, I saw him on the street. He had another piece of trash with him.'

'Umm, I saw him too. It was hard to tell whether he was the same kind of man as Hamilton or just an ordinary cowhand. But from first glance I agree with you.' Chapman was worried. Alice was the nearest in the way. His only hope was that Wallace would be reluctant to fight a woman and would come to realize that he had more than enough land for his needs. Unfortunately, he thought it was a slim hope. 'If only Patterson would do something.'

'Some chance! Fred is a good town marshal but that's all he is. Anyway he has no authority for what happens out on the range.'

'And quite wisely he also has no desire to go up against either Wallace, who is wealthy and powerful, or Hamilton, who is just powerful.' All Chapman felt he could do was repeat his earlier warning. 'Be careful, I don't want to see you hurt.'

'You might follow your own advice.' Alice picked up a copy of *The Enquirer,* whose editorial, written like the rest of the paper by Chapman, contained another attack on Richard Wallace. It didn't mention names but there was no doubt as to who was meant by "the wolf in sheep's clothing coming into our peaceful community to create havoc". 'I doubt whether Wallace will approve of your criticism.'

'I'm like you, Alice. I can't sit back and keep quiet. Fairmont used to be a nice, peaceful town with a good future for itself and the surrounding community. Now no one knows what's going to happen. You know, I've spent most of my life travelling around, setting up newspapers wherever I've stopped. Some didn't last much longer than a month, or they died when the town did, some I passed on to others for them to continue. I was always proudest of *The Enquirer*. It had something to say and a decent place and decent people to say it about. And because of that I've stayed here five years, which is the longest I've stayed anywhere. I found myself caring. I'm not so sure any longer.'

'I hope you don't go.'

'Oh, don't worry, I've no intention of leaving until this is all sorted out. After that, who knows?'

Chapman took off his round spectacles and rubbed his eyes. He glanced at the

43

young widow, wondering if this was the right time to say it really all depended on her. That if she agreed that maybe sometime in the future there might be a possibility she could come to love him, then, of course, he'd stay. He decided against speaking out. Her husband hadn't been dead for long, she naturally still mourned and missed him. And there was the difference in their ages. He was in his forties, whereas she was twenty-eight. They were good friends, that was enough for now, he didn't want to risk spoiling what they had.

Sighing a little at his cowardice, he hooked his glasses back on. 'Where's Billy?'

Alice's face softened. 'With Mrs McGee. She loves looking after him and luckily he likes being with her. I sometimes think it would be fairer to leave him here with her so he'd have children of his own age to play with.'

Knowing that would mean Alice coming into town more often to visit her son and thus giving Chapman a chance to see her, he almost agreed. But Alice loved Billy very much and would hate to be parted from him. She didn't want any more sadness in her life.

'I'm sure he's better off with you. Still it's a comfort to know that if necessary Mrs McGee would look after him for you. And now, Alice, what do you say to accompanying me over to the cafe and joining me for lunch? I believe Mr Reynolds is cooking a nice beef stew today.'

'My, my, what a surprise.'

Mr Reynolds always cooked beef stew.

'Come along then.'

## FOUR

It didn't take Forbes long to realize that Ira Hamilton wasn't the most popular man ever to set foot in Fairmont. And because Forbes was with him, the hostility spread to him. Wherever they went he was aware of sullen looks and surly tones. About the only place they'd been welcomed in was here, the Bull's Head Saloon. That was partly because the rest of the clientele wasn't up to much either and partly because, whatever their personal feelings might be, the bartenders and the girls were paid to be polite to all their customers.

When Forbes asked Hamilton about the town's unfriendliness, by way of explanation, Ira said, 'They don't like anyone who works for Mr Wallace and they don't like Mr Wallace because he's taking a stand against the rustlers. Also he's from the East and has a lot of money. They're jealous. Christ, you've only got to read the garbage that newspaper editor prints to know that.' He threw a copy of *The Enquirer* down on the table. 'Look at that goddamned nonsense.'

Forbes turned the paper around so that the headline faced him but said nothing.

The foreman paused to drink some of his beer, before picking up the paper again. 'You'd think a fairly intelligent man like Casey Chapman would either print the truth or keep quiet wouldn't you? Not make up lies. Still it seems like he sees a lot of Alice Munroe, even spends time out there at her place, and her on her own an' all, you know what I mean?' Hamilton grinned.

Forbes grinned back. He knew exactly what Hamilton was getting at.

'So maybe he's doing it to impress her and try to get even more friendly.'

'Has anyone caused any real trouble yet?'

'No.' Hamilton didn't sound all that happy. 'Most of 'em have been like the Deanes and taken heed of Mr Wallace's warnings and taken also Mr Wallace's money. The bastards that are left are different. Most of them don't really understand anything except force.' Pausing, he added casually, 'Will it worry you if we do have to go up against 'em?'

'Not if we're given reason.'

'Don't worry. I reckon whatever we do, it'll be in self-defence.'

Forbes wasn't particularly reassured. Hamilton could simply mean that he'd somehow fix it to look like the rustlers had been the ones to shoot first. He turned to signal one of the saloongirls to bring him another beer. 'Do you want one, Ira?'

'No. I think I'll wander over to The Star. A couple of gals are singing there tonight. Then I'm going onto a brothel. What about you?'

Forbes jingled the money in his pockets. He'd already bought a new shirt, jacket and a pair of socks, as well as some bullets. He reckoned that the rest of his money was his to do with what he wanted, which was have a good time, although doubtless that hadn't been what Hamilton had had in mind for him to spend it on. 'Guess I'll stay here.' This place was much more to his liking than the fancy Star, with its silver and gold decorations and sweet singing girls. The Bull's Head had little in the way of decoration and the girls surely weren't interested in singing. 'Maybe gamble a little.'

'Well don't cheat!' Hamilton warned ominously. 'And it might not be a bad idea to stay reasonably sober. It's a long ride back to the ranch.'

'Don't worry, I know when to stop,' Forbes boasted, not exactly accurately.

Hamilton stood up, threw a dollar at the girl who'd served them, and went out.

Forbes was relieved to see him go. Now to spend an hour or so doing what he liked, without being watched and told what to do all the time. However, the evening didn't quite turn out in the way he hoped.

For, despite his boast to Hamilton, he drank far too much, passed out in the middle of a card game and had to be thrown out of the saloon by its two bruisers. He landed face down in the muddy street. Once in the cold night air he woke up and managed to stagger about a bit before falling over and going to sleep under the sidewalk.

And that was where he was woken the following morning by someone giving him a hefty kick in the ribs.

Groaning, Forbes opened his eyes as far

as he could. Head thumping, he stared up at the bulky figure outlined against the early morning sun and saw winking back at him a marshal's silver badge.

'Oh God,' he moaned.

'Get up you piece of scum! Who the hell do you think you are littering up the streets like this? Come on, move yourself!'

'All right, all right.' Somewhat theatrically Forbes placed a hand over his eyes and managed to lever himself into a sitting position.

But the Marshal gave no kindly consideration to how he felt. Reaching out he grabbed hold of Forbes' arm jerking him to his feet.

Wondering if he was going to be sick, Forbes swayed unsteadily for a moment or two. Desperately he clung hold of the saloon post until the universe settled back into its normal orbit.

'Listen, son,' the Marshal poked him in the chest, 'I don't want scum like you coming into my town behaving like this! I won't do anything about you this time because you obviously didn't know I have certain rules for people to follow but if you get so drunk you pass out in the street again you're gonna wake up in jail and stay there too!'

Forbes belched loudly. 'Yeah sure, Marshal.' He didn't take a great deal of notice. Over the years he'd been warned by the law many times and in more forcible ways than this.

'Have you got any money? Or a job?'

'Yeah. I'm working for Mr Wallace at the Rocking W.'

Marshal Patterson's eyes narrowed. 'Really? Well you certainly don't look like a cowboy. And I don't want any trouble from hired gunhands, just remember that too. Now go on, get outta here. Go sober up.'

This being good advice, Forbes staggered down the street towards the livery stable where he could stick his aching head into the trough of cold water. He was aware of those he passed giving him looks that told him only too clearly that they didn't think much of him. That was all right.

He really didn't think much of himself either.

Later on, hair hanging wetly round his face, whiskers sprouting from his chin, Forbes went back to the saloon. Seeing as how he had been such a good customer the night before, the bartender didn't charge him for gulping down what seemed like several gallons of black coffee. After that Forbes felt, if didn't look, a bit better. He'd arranged to meet Hamilton at the Food and Grain Store at 10 o'clock but first he had to pick up his personal purchases and buy some tobacco.

Mrs Someone or Other, the woman Hamilton had greeted the day before and who was misbehaving with the newspaper editor, was in the store. She was chatting to the owner and a pretty young girl with dark hair hanging in waves halfway down her back.

With Mrs Someone or Other was a small boy of about six. Forbes regarded him warily. He didn't like or understand children; they were a foreign species to him. The boy looked back at him in exactly the same way.

Both women and the store clerk fell silent at his entrance and he was uncomfortably aware of them staring at him as he shuffled towards the counter. The woman turned up her nose and quickly stepped out of the way, standing in front of the girl as if afraid he was going to attack her in broad daylight or something.

Well, perhaps he wasn't looking at his best this morning, but there was no need for her to be so snooty. She wasn't exactly a picture of beauty herself with her brown hair pulled back from her face and tied up in an unflattering bun, a tanned face—even Forbes knew that a lady should have pale skin—and a shabby skirt and shapeless jacket. What was more her morals didn't sound all that good either.

What gave her the right to criticise him?

Now the other girl was much easier on the eye, although she was too young and innocent for the likes of Forbes. That didn't stop him from looking at her appreciatively.

'Good morning ladies,' he said and touched the brim of his hat.

Forbes renamed the woman 'Mrs Snooty' as she sniffed haughtily at him. On purpose he belched long and loudly, almost laughing at the look of disgust that showed on her face.

'Here you are,' the store clerk said quickly, handing him his purchases from the day before, obviously in a hurry to get rid of him.

'Ladies,' Forbes said again and was so glad to get away from their sneering faces that he forgot all about buying his tobacco. Snobs, he thought and slammed the door shut behind him, well aware that they were going to talk about him.

Forbes was right. He'd no sooner gone than Alice Munroe turned to the store clerk. 'You'd better let me have some more of those shotgun shells, Bert, I've a feeling I'm going to need them.'

'Oh dear, Mrs Munroe,' Laura Reynolds said, 'is he the one you said was with Ira Hamilton? I didn't like the look of him at all.'

'Nor did I. Don't worry I can handle bums like him. He's the sort of drunken cowardly bully who, faced with a show of force, even from a woman, will turn tail and run.' Or at least that was what Alice hoped.

'I'll walk you to the buckboard, Mrs Munroe. Come on Billy.' Laura took the boy's hand and together they went out of the store while Alice paid what she owed. The buckboard waited outside, the horse hitched up and ready to go, the stores loaded in the back. Laura picked the boy up and swung him round in her arms and then up onto the seat. Billy smiled but as usual he didn't laugh or say anything. Laura felt sad. Billy had been such a happy boy and now he was always so serious with a faraway look in his eyes.

As Alice came out of the store she saw that Hamilton and the drunk had met up across the road at the Food and Grain Store. They appeared to be arguing but that didn't stop Hamilton from glancing over at Laura every now and again. Alice wasn't pleased. Laura was a lovely looking girl with a bright personality. She couldn't help but attract men. Alice knew they looked at her in vain. All Laura had thoughts and hopes for was young Paul Broome. She noticed and wanted no one else. But that wouldn't stop the likes of Hamilton and the thought of him pressing his attentions on Laura made Alice both angry and distressed.

'Do you know if Paul is coming into town soon?' Laura asked as Alice came up to her.

'He's very busy at his father's ranch at the moment. I'm sure he'll come in when he can. If I see him can I tell him anything?'

'You could give him this.' Laura drew a blue envelope scented with violets out of her jacket pocket and gave it to Alice.

'All right. I'll see he gets it.'

'Thanks.' Laura kissed Alice and then kissed Billy. 'I'd better go. Pa needs help in the cafe.' And she tripped away down the street.

Scowling across at Hamilton, Alice

climbed up onto the buckboard seat. 'Let's go home, Billy.'

'Yes, Ma.' Billy clutched his mother's hand.

'She's too young for you,' said Forbes, who had also noticed Hamilton's glances over at the two women.

'Who? Oh, Laura Reynolds you mean? It ain't her I'm looking at. It's the other one.'

Well, Forbes thought, Mrs Snooty must have something about her if she attracted both the newspaper editor and Ira Hamilton but damned if he could see what it was.

'You look like you took on a skinful last night. Thought I told you not to get drunk.'

'Don't start again,' Forbes protested. 'I've felt worse. I'll be OK by the time we get back to the ranch.'

Hamilton didn't look as if he believed him. 'Let's go then. There's plenty to do once we get there.'

That was what Forbes was afraid of.

# FIVE

Forbes' fear of hard work was soon realized. First off Wallace, following Hamilton's advice, agreed that some of the cattle should be moved up to the North Pasture, where the grass was fresh and green.

'Del and Burt can't do that on their own,' Ira told Forbes, 'so we've got to help. It'll also be a good opportunity for me to show you some of Wallace's land. So pack some extra food and a warm shirt and spare pair of socks, it'll be cold up in the hills.'

Forbes, who was quite used to spending time out in the open for one reason or another, rather resented being told what to do. 'How long we going to be out?'

'Only a few days. There's too much to do around the ranch to be away longer. 'Course there ain't no way you can see all of the ranch in that time but we'll be able to look at some of the places where the rustlers have struck so far.'

Forbes couldn't say he liked getting up early and riding all day in the saddle chasing after cows who were reluctant to go where they were meant to. Long dusty hours, Hamilton giving out his orders and poor trail food, cooked by Burt. He didn't even have time for a drink. It wasn't how he'd meant to spend the Spring.

But at last the cattle were in their new home and could be left safely in the hands of the two young cowboys.

'And keep a sharp look out,' Hamilton warned. 'If anyone comes close shoot first and then see what they want. Don't take any risks.'

'We won't,' Del said.

'Stay here for a few days until the cattle are settled in and then you can come back to the ranch.'

Once Forbes and Hamilton left the lowland meadows behind, it turned much colder, making Forbes glad of his new thick jacket. There was still a lot of snow on the mountains and some remained in the shady spots under the pine trees, while the edges of the creeks were thick with ice. During the day the sun came out but so far up in the hills it had little warmth to it.

Groups of cows huddled together here and there and Hamilton inspected them all. 'Look,' he said on more than one occasion, pointing to the ground. While Forbes nodded knowledgeably, he couldn't make out anything except a jumble of indistinguishable hoofmarks.

Evidently though, they meant a lot to Hamilton, because he said, 'Seems the bastards have been busy since Mr Wallace and I went East to buy those beeves. There's plenty of tracks from two, three weeks back and it looks to me like several cows and calves have disappeared. They could have wandered away but more likely they've been rustled.'

'Are there any tracks we can follow?'

'Not any more. Even if there was, any evidence would have long gone. The cows have probably been slaughtered for food by now and the calves will be mavericks waiting to have the wrong brand put on 'em. It'll mean that Mr Wallace won't have as many cows as he should to send to market while all of a sudden the sodbusters are doing well.'

During their ride, Forbes could see how easy it would be for rustlers to strike against Richard Wallace. He had so much land and during the winter months, the cattle, left mostly to their own devices, had wandered all over it. And now Wallace didn't have enough men to patrol it. No wonder he was willing to pay him, and Hamilton, such good wages; they were each doing the work of five men!

They had almost got back to the ranch when riding to the top of the high ridge they were following, they saw below them some twenty or so beeves being driven along by two men.

Hamilton reached out a hand, signalling Forbes to stop. 'The Broomes, father and son.'

'Who are they?'

'Just about the worst of the bunch that's left. Been here years and think

61

they can do what they like. I reckon they've always rustled the odd beef or two, especially when times were hard. They probably don't think they're doing anything wrong. And since Mr Wallace's arrival they've seen him and his ranch as easy pickings.' Hamilton laughed. 'They're gonna find out different, real soon.'

'How many of 'em are there?' Forbes asked, thinking it was always best to know your enemy before you went up against them.

'Broome and the kid, Paul, down there. Real hothead he is. Out to cause trouble.' Hamilton sounded as if he'd like it fine if young Broome started the trouble with him. 'Sparking that pretty little Laura Reynolds. Then there's the wife and two small girls.'

'Think if we ride down there we'll find any of Mr Wallace's cattle amongst that lot?'

'Doubt it. If they intended to keep any of the cows, first thing they'd have done would be to change the brand. Still even so it might be best if we showed 'em we know what they're up to.'

Forbes was afraid Hamilton had been going to say that.

'Come on.'

As they rode down the ridge towards the cattle, Broome and his son stopped to turn and stare. There was no liking on their faces and Paul's hand dropped towards the Colt on his hip. Hamilton said nothing but, while Forbes waited off to one side, rode slowly up and down the small herd, making sure the Broomes knew he was staring at the brands.

'What do you want here?' George Broome demanded. 'This ain't Wallace's property and it ain't Wallace's herd.'

Hamilton brought his horse up close to Broome's and stared across at the man in his usual hard eyed way. 'Just making sure.'

'Well, are you sure?'

'Yeah but not satisfied.'

'These are our cattle,' Paul said. 'And you damn well know it.'

'Where you taking 'em?'

'None of your damn business,' Paul declared.

But Broome, seeing Hamilton's hand inching towards his gun, said, 'We're trying to gather some of 'em up is all. Getting a start on Spring round up.'

'You going to help Mrs Munroe when the time comes?'

'Someone has to.'

'Might be best if you didn't. She's a troublemaker. Wouldn't want you tarred with the same brush.'

'Might be best if you minded your own business,' Paul said rudely.

'Might also be best if you minded your manners, kid.'

'Perhaps you'd like to teach me.'

'Paul,' Broome warned.

Hamilton laughed. 'You're so eager ain't you, kid, maybe one day I'll make your dreams come true and take you up on your offer.'

'Any time, Mr Hamilton, I'll be ready.'

'Oh, go on, get outta here.' Hamilton laughed again, making Paul go red with anger. 'Just take my warning and be careful.'

Neither Broome said anything as they urged their horses forward and continued driving their cows down the track.

Hamilton laughed again. 'That kid is sure asking for a good beating, or worse,' he said to Forbes.

'And I just bet you'd like to give it to him.'

'Sure would, Forbes, sure would! Now let's get on back to the ranch. I want to tell the boss about all we've seen.'

Richard Wallace wasn't hard to convince that Hamilton was right. He sat facing his two men, his hands steepled under his chin. It was the first time Forbes had actually been allowed into the house. He had never seen anything quite like the study before, and wondered if he was showing himself up by gaping at all the luxuries.

The furniture was dark leather, a thick carpet covered the floor. Over an enormous fireplace hung a rifle and a buffalo's head, while more sporting trophies and sporting paintings decorated the other walls. Facing the desk was a portrait of a stern looking man with huge whiskers; evidently Richard Wallace's father. Forbes noticed Wallace kept glancing at it, as if scared of doing something wrong and being reprimanded.

'What do you advise ought to be done? It doesn't seem there's enough proof that my cattle have been rustled to go to the law. Yet you're sure they haven't just wandered away?'

'I'm sure, Mr Wallace. And the Broomes seem the most likely culprits.'

'I agree. Then perhaps what happened to the Deanes should happen to the Broomes, with hopefully the same result.'

'Yes, sir.'

'What did he mean?' Forbes asked as Hamilton went back to the bunkhouse with him.

'Just this.' The foreman handed Forbes a piece of paper. 'I want you to take this and pin it up on the Broomes' door.'

'What is it?'

The words on the paper were printed

in thick black ink and Hamilton quoted them as if by heart: 'Rustlers, thieves and vagabonds—this is your last chance—leave or face the consequences.'

Forbes almost sniggered. He bet Hamilton had written that and all by himself. The sentiment wasn't very original. Such notices were always being pinned up to clear places of undesirables. Strangely enough they often succeeded in what they set out to do and the outlaws targetted did as they were warned and left.

'Why should I be the one to go?'

'Because I'm the one that gives out the orders and you're the one who takes 'em.'

Before he left that night to ride to the Broomes, Forbes had several swallows of whiskey. Then with a shrug he put the bottle in his pocket. Why not? The past few nights with Hamilton keeping a careful eye on him, there hadn't been any opportunity for a drink. Life was in danger of getting too damn serious; and it wasn't like he'd have too much.

# SIX

After a while George Broome took pity on his son and said that as they'd moved the cattle quickly, he could go into town. Paul worked long hours and didn't have much spare time but what he did he spent with Laura, despite the lengthy journey involved. He hadn't managed to get to Fairmont for a couple of weeks now and wanted to see Laura again, moping around all day with a soppy look on his face, tossing and turning half of the night, making him more or less useless.

'Are you sure, Pa?' Paul asked dutifully. 'What about Hamilton?'

'Oh I doubt he's around any longer. He wanted to cause mischief he wouldn't have waited. Go on be off with you. Try not to be back too late. You know how your Ma worries.'

Paul needed no second bidding. He

turned his horse's head, dug heels into its side and sent it off at a gallop towards Fairmont.

By the time he got there it was already late afternoon. He left his animal to be cared for at the livery and then hurried along the sidewalks to the cafe. It was empty when he got there; too late for lunch diners, too early for those wanting an evening meal. Mr Reynolds was behind the counter, shuffling dollar bills, and Laura was laying tables.

'Paul!' she squealed as she saw who had come in. Running up to him she hugged him tightly.

'Hallo, sweetheart,' Paul said, a silly grin on his face. Aware of Mr Reynolds watching, he pushed her away and gave her a decorous kiss on the cheek.

A pink glow about her face, Laura lowered her eyes so her father wouldn't see the happiness in them. Paul was eighteen and had curly brown hair and brown eyes. He had just about grown out of the gangling arms and legs stage and was of middling height, with a broad chest and muscled arms. Laura was thrilled that someone as good looking as he was should notice her.

'May we go out for a short walk, Mr Reynolds?' Paul asked politely.

Despite the careful way in which the youngsters were behaving, Reynolds had as good an idea as George Broome of what they got up to when they were alone. He wasn't quite so unconcerned about it as Broome. After all Laura was his daughter and he feared all the hazards that could await her. He sighed. Being a father to a young girl, with no mother, wasn't easy. Still Paul was a trustworthy young man and Reynolds knew better than to try to keep them apart.

'All right,' he agreed. 'But don't be too long, Laura. And take your coat, it's cold out there.'

Hamilton sat on the edge of his bunk, smoking and reading a dime novel. Not that he was taking in the words. He was busy thinking about the situation, and wondering what to do about it, because he wasn't satisfied. He was exceedingly disgruntled. Pinning notices on doors was all very well. But it either meant that the family targetted left, like the Deanes, or stayed and whined on about their innocence, like the Broomes would. And then what? When would Wallace agree to taking the matter further?

Talk, talk! What Hamilton wanted, and had expected, was action. What was the good of threatening the sodbusters if the threat was never carried out?

Putting down the book, he stared into space. Perhaps there was something he could do to force Mr Wallace to act. Suddenly he grinned. Now, why the hell hadn't he thought of that before?

'I'll have to go soon. I won't get home before it's dark as it is.'

'I wish you didn't have to.'

'So do I.'

Paul and Laura lay in one another's arms down by their favourite secluded spot by the river. This early in the year the ground was still damp and the air cold, but neither fact worried the youngsters. Nothing bothered them, except each other.

He kissed her again and for a moment or two they clung together, unwilling to let one another go. Then reluctantly he pushed the girl away and sat up. 'I must go. And so must you. Your pa will want help with the evening meal. He'll also wonder where we've got to.'

'I know.' Laura got to her feet, shaking out her skirts. 'I wish we could be together forever. And I wish there wasn't all this trouble with that horrible Mr Wallace. You won't do anything silly, will you Paul? I couldn't bear it if anything happened to you.'

Paul laughed. At his age and with all his life in front of him, he had no fears. 'Don't worry, sweetheart, nothing's going to happen to me. I can take care of myself.'

Laura said nothing. Paul had a quick temper and she was scared he would do something foolish. She considered Paul better than any other man she knew, but she wasn't quite so blind not to realize that he would be no match for the foreman's strength and speed.

Hand in hand they walked back to the livery stable. There they kissed again and said goodbye. Laura waited and waved to Paul until he turned the corner by the barn and was lost to sight.

Although Paul had wanted to be home before it was fully dark, he had lingered so long with Laura that shadows had stretched across the ground before he was halfway there. He passed the turn off to Mrs Munroe's place. Not far now. Only a few more miles down the road.

And suddenly he pulled his horse to a halt. Hoofbeats were approaching him. A ridden horse.

Normally Paul wouldn't have been frightened. After all anyone could be out here: someone going into town as he was returning, a stray cowboy. He told himself he wasn't frightened now. It was simply commonsense to be careful. So he turned the horse off the road, back amongst the scrub, and leaned forward in the saddle, urging it to be quiet.

A few moments later the other rider came into view. It was light enough for Paul to recognize him. It was the new hand, who'd been out with Ira Hamilton earlier. Forbes, Laura had said his name was. And from the way he was swaying in the saddle he was almost as drunk as Laura said he'd been in town. Maybe he would fall off and be left afoot—serve him right! Wallace must be desperate to employ someone like that. Paul wondered what he was doing out here.

Once Forbes had ridden by, Paul continued on his journey and soon saw the reason for the man's night escapade.

'Look at this!' he shouted, bursting through the door into the room beyond, where his parents sat at the table, having just finished their supper. He threw down a piece of paper. 'That was pinned to the door. How dare they? Rustlers, thieves, vagabonds! How dare they call us that?'

George and Norah Broome stared at one another in dismay. The bedroom door opened and Judith and Rachel, Paul's young sisters, peered out, sleepy eyed yet attracted by the noise.

'What are we meant to have done now that Wallace is going to falsely accuse us of?' Paul demanded, so angry that he couldn't stand still.

'We don't have to have done anything for Wallace to make a move like this,' Broome replied.

'Perhaps we ought to go while we can,' Norah spoke tearfully.

'No!' Paul shouted. 'We ain't done anything, we ain't going.'

'I'm only thinking of your sisters. They could get hurt.'

'I know, Ma, but why should we go? We're not rustlers or thieves.'

Paul looked at his parents. Their difficult lives showed on their faces, especially his mother's. Her skin was lined, with wrinkles round eyes and mouth, hair already turning grey. They had never had much in the way of anything that wasn't necessary. But what they had was their own. And now, when they were in a position to begin enjoying some monetary reward for all their efforts and should be looking forward to a slightly easier time, here was Richard Wallace coming to pile more worries on their heads.

Paul also had himself to think of. This ranch would be his one day. Sometimes in the past he'd dreamt of running away and becoming an army scout or a gold miner, but no longer. Now he loved Laura and wanted to provide a good home for her and the family they'd have. Wallace wasn't going to take that away from him, not if Paul could help it.

'Wallace will use this,' Paul indicated the threatening notice, 'so he doesn't even need to offer to buy us out. He'll march in and take over. But not without a fight he ain't going to. Damn him.'

'Mind your language,' Norah said automatically.

'This time Wallace might find that whatever he tries he'll be trying too much,' Paul said with a determined look in his eyes.

# SEVEN

The following morning when Forbes eventually got up, he found himself alone at the ranch. Del and Burt were still at the North Pasture and when Forbes went outside to see why Hamilton hadn't come to roust him out of bed, the foreman had gone off on his horse doing something on his own.

Forbes was thankful. His eyes were a bit unfocussed, his head ached and his mouth felt furry. Perhaps he shouldn't have drunk so much the night before. There were jobs to be done, but feeling so bad, and as he rarely did any work unless someone was there to supervise him, he decided instead to laze around the bunkhouse. Part of the time he thought about his unexpected change of circumstances.

While he wasn't all that sure about the job, it not being usual for him to be on the side of the law, it was well paid, the ranch was comfortable and the work so far appeared reasonably easy, so long as it didn't involve much more riding around. He'd stay for the summer at least. After that he'd see. Probably once the rustling was sorted out, Wallace wouldn't want to employ him any longer; Forbes knew only too well that he wasn't here because he was a brilliant cowhand. Anyway Forbes didn't like to stay in the same place too long. He might well want to move on himself.

He was just closing his eyes going to sleep when Richard Wallace came in. Jerking upright, Forbes tried to pretend he was actually doing something, although he didn't really imagine he'd fooled his boss.

'Ira around?'

'No, sir. He's gone out checking on things.'

'You'll do then. Come with me.'

'Where we going?'

'To see Mrs Munroe.'

Ah yes, that was the name of Mrs Snooty.

'Mrs Munroe owns the ranch next to

mine,' Wallace explained as the two men rode along side by side. 'I've been trying to buy it since I got here. It would make sense for me to have it.'

'Perhaps she thinks it makes more sense for her to keep it.'

Wallace frowned. 'But I'd be doing her a favour. She's a widow and what do women know about ranching? By staying on all she's doing is getting herself deeper and deeper into trouble, both at the ranch and at the bank in town. If she accepts my offer she'll be able to pay off all her debts and still have enough to move some place where she can start anew in a job more suited to a woman. I daresay she'd make a good enough seamstress, or something like that. Today I intend to increase my offer.'

'Do you think she'll accept?'

'I doubt it. Mrs Munroe is very stubborn. However, she will come round to my way of thinking in the end.'

Was that a threat? Forbes didn't much like the idea of threatening a woman, even a snooty one like Mrs Munroe.

But Wallace was smiling as he spoke so perhaps it wasn't.

'Is she involved with the rustlers?'

'Not any more.' Wallace didn't elaborate on what he meant. 'But she goes around stirring everyone else up against me. I don't know why. I've never done anything to upset her.'

'Probably just in her nature.' Forbes had known a number of women like that.

Forbes might not understand Wallace and they were certainly miles apart in their ways of life, but he had to agree with one thing he said: women didn't know anything about running a ranch. A view reinforced by his first look at the Munroe place.

Clustered near the fast running stream they'd been following for the last few miles were several buildings. A house, small but sturdy, with glass in the windows, an overgrown vegetable garden off to one side, and a barn and a corral all grouped round an untidy yard. Over everything hung an air of dereliction. There were holes in the sides of the barn, the corral walls needed repair and weeds sprouted up everywhere.

The only thing well tended was the grave on the slight rise overlooking the house. Some early flowers were placed on it and there was a fancy headstone. As Wallace didn't remark on it neither did Forbes but he supposed as Mrs Snooty was a widow it likely contained the remains of her husband.

The shame of it was that the land was so good. There would always be water, the grass along the riverbank was tall and thick. Even in the long hot summers the nearby hills would provide upland meadows as well as shelter in the winter.

Forbes could understand why Richard Wallace wanted to buy the land if not the buildings. He couldn't understand why a woman would want to cling on, all alone, out here.

As he and Wallace crossed the river and rode up into the yard, the door to the house opened and Alice Munroe came out to stand in the mud.

Forbes experienced two shocks.

First, while she had one hand resting on the shoulder of her small son, in the crook of her other arm she carried a shotgun. Forbes glanced nervously at Wallace. He didn't think that women knew how to fire guns, not properly, but with a shotgun that didn't matter. All you had to do was aim in your target's general direction and pull the trigger.

But his other shock was even greater than the fact that she'd welcomed them carrying a gun. As in town she had her hair pulled back in an unflattering bun and today was wearing a check shirt and boots—and pants! Not a skirt, not even a divided skirt, but pants and men's pants at that!

Forbes could hardly take his eyes off such a disgusting sight. Men's pants! No woman with even the slightest pretence of being a lady would wear trousers. And then she'd dared look at him as if he was a bug crawling beneath her feet. How was Wallace taking this startling sight? But he must have been used to it for all he did was politely remove his hat and nod in her direction.

'Hold it right there,' Alice said sharply.

'And don't bother to get off your horses, you're not stopping.'

'Now, now there's no need to be like that. I'm only here to...'

'There's every need to be like that,' Alice interrupted. 'And I know exactly what you're here for. To try and steal my property.'

'I'm not trying to steal anything,' Wallace said in an amazed and annoyed tone. 'I'm here to make you a good offer.'

'And I've told you more than once that I don't want to sell. I wish you'd get that through your thick head.'

Wallace's handsome face flushed with annoyance at her rudeness but his tone remained reasonable as he said, 'Look around, Mrs Munroe, if you don't sell all I'll have to do is wait and take it from you.'

'Then that's what I suggest you do.'

'Don't take that tone. We're neighbours and neighbours should help one another.'

'All you ever do is help yourself, Mr Wallace.' For the first time Alice looked at Forbes. It still seemed as if she didn't like what she saw. 'Did you really think it necessary to come out here with your new gunhand? Were you too scared to face me on your own? Or perhaps you thought that I'd be so impressed by him that I'd throw up my hands in horror and give you the deeds to the ranch here and now? Let me tell you, Mr Wallace, there was nothing particularly impressive or frightening about him when I saw him drunk and sleeping it off under the town sidewalk!'

Forbes went red and refused to look at his boss, who didn't mind drink but didn't approve of drunks. The bitch! Giving him away like that! He hadn't done anything to her. And what did she mean by gunhand? All right, so he wasn't exactly an ordinary cowboy but so far he hadn't gone round shooting up the town!

'I really don't know what you're talking about,' Wallace said, on his dignity. 'Won't you invite us in so that we can talk things over? I'm willing to up my offer by five dollars an acre.'

'I don't care how much you offer, my ranch isn't for sale. Now, why don't you

84

leave while you can?'

'Is that a threat?'

'Of course it is.'

'Oh!' Wallace said angrily. 'I can see you're in one of your moods and that it's of little use trying to make you listen to me. I'll come back when you're more amenable.'

'In that case, Mr Wallace, you needn't bother coming back.' Alice pushed Billy behind her and raised the shotgun slightly. 'Get off my land and take your drunk with you!'

Wallace didn't speak on the ride back to the ranch and Forbes didn't say anything either. His boss was red faced with annoyance and had a set look to his mouth. He was finding out that his good looks and Eastern charm didn't always work and he clearly didn't like being rebuffed in front of one of his hands, especially by a woman. Yet Wallace must have known that Mrs Munroe was likely to react like that so why take him along? Was it for a show of force as she'd accused?

Forbes couldn't believe that. Wallace

had done nothing except talk to her. He'd made no threatening moves. Nor had he asked Forbes to do anything either. Mrs Snooty had been the one threatening to use the shotgun. Wallace had to be right. Mrs Snooty was just being stubborn and silly. Forbes was quite prepared to believe anything of a woman who wore men's pants!

'Ma,' Billy looked up at his mother.

'It's all right, dear, they've gone, 'Alice reassured him but nevertheless she kept the shotgun with her as she walked to the corral and watched the dust of the men's horses as they disappeared in the meadow beyond the river.

For a moment she slumped against the split rail fence, her problems seeming to overwhelm her. What was she going to do? The place needed repairs she could neither afford nor do herself. She was all alone. If it wasn't for the help of her nearest neighbours, the Broomes, she'd never be able to manage. And there was always the threat of violence against her.

Why didn't she take the advice of Casey, of everyone else, and sell to Richard Wallace? It wasn't as if he was trying to cheat her. He was offering a good price. Even though it wouldn't be easy for a woman of her age with a small son to look after, to start again, it wouldn't be that difficult either. Not any more difficult than staying here anyway.

But looking across at Billy, she knew she had to stay. This was all for him. With his corn coloured hair and blue eyes he was so like his father it was enough to make her cry.

She and William had worked hard to make the ranch a success. The birth of their son had delighted them both. All she'd ever wanted had been her's. Well that was all different now. The good times were over and could never return. But that didn't mean she had to consider depriving Billy of his legacy.

Besides it wasn't just that William was dead. He'd been murdered.

And there was no way she was going to sell out to the bastard responsible.

# EIGHT

'Sir! Mr Wallace!'

Forbes and Wallace had almost reached the ranch headquarters when a fast riding horseman came towards them, waving his hat and yelling. They stopped. Within minutes Ira Hamilton reached them, pulling his horse to a halt in a dust cloud that made Wallace fussily brush down his jacket.

'What is it?' the rancher demanded.

'Burt just rode in from the North Pasture. About five cows are missing. They only went this morning. We hurry we might pick up a fresh trail.'

Wallace looked excited. 'Then I suggest you get going.'

'Yes, sir! C'mon Forbes!'

Together the two men returned to the ranch so that Forbes could pick out a fresh mount. Then leaving Burt behind to get something to eat, and being waved off by Wallace, they started out. Hamilton set a fast pace but even so they didn't get to the North Pasture until evening shadows were lengthening across the ground and Del had supper cooking over a smokey fire.

'Mind telling me what happened?' Hamilton demanded, accepting a cup of vile looking coffee. 'You were meant to be here guarding the cattle, not losing 'em.'

'It weren't our fault,' Del moaned. 'It was lucky we didn't get ourselves shot.'

'What happened?' Hamilton repeated.

'When me and Burt got up this morning we noticed that the cattle were restless. We saw that about five cows were missing. They must have been taken in the night.'

'But you didn't hear anything?'

'No.'

'Or seen anything more?'

Del shook his head. 'Whoever took 'em has long gone. They won't be back.'

'You're sure the cattle were stolen?' Forbes asked. 'Why couldn't they have just wandered away?'

'We didn't go off half cock. We searched

all round and found some tracks. They lead towards the rocks on the far side of the pasture.'

'Towards the Broomes,' Hamilton nodded in satisfaction. 'It's too late to go following the trail tonight. Forbes and me'll start off first thing in the morning while you stay here with the cattle, Del.'

'Sure thing, Ira.'

'You any good at tracking, Forbes?'

'Not really.' Forbes was quite good at hiding his tracks from pursuing lawmen, he'd never had a lot of call to follow a trail.

'Well don't matter much. We know where they're going.'

'So you say.' Ira was probably right about the Broomes. In Forbes' limited experience of homesteaders, poor dirt scrabble farmers often thought rustling from those better off was a legitimate occupation. But to his mind Ira was just a bit too eager to find them guilty.

'Yeah, I do say.' Hamilton glared at him. 'Don't go soft on me, Forbes. You're getting good money for the little you've done so far.'

'Don't worry about me. I know exactly what I'm getting paid for.'

The next morning in a bit of a hostile silence, the two men rode across the pasture. Their breath was white on the cold air and the ground was covered with a slowly lifting mist, that made everything seem quieter than it already was. In the rocks they lost any obvious sign of the cattle but beyond, on the soft ground leading to the valley below, the trail was easy to see. Even Forbes could make out that there were five or six cattle, driven by one horseman, who was making no attempt to hide the tracks.

When Forbes mentioned this, Hamilton shrugged. 'Like most outlaws, the Broomes ain't any too smart. Perhaps they didn't think anyone would bother following 'em.'

'Perhaps it ain't gonna be the Broomes after all. Or maybe someone is trying to make out it's them when it ain't.'

'Why should anyone do that? Anyway

that's the Broomes' land down there.'
Hamilton pointed to the far end of the
valley which even at this distance was
clearly fenced off. 'And that's where the
cattle are being driven. But OK maybe
I'm wrong and the tracks will turn off
soon, we'll see.'

Hamilton wasn't wrong. The tracks led
in a more or less straight line up the
middle of the narrow valley and crossed
through a broken gap in the fence.

'How convenient,' Hamilton sneered.
'Now Broome can say that the cattle
must have wandered onto his land all
by themselves and that it wasn't anything
to do with him.'

A short way beyond the fence they came
to a copse of trees and bushes. In a clearing
in the middle was evidence of a small fire
having recently been left to die.

Hamilton dismounted and walked up to
the fire, inspecting the ashes. 'Looks to me
like some branding has been going on.
The Rocking W has been changed into
the Lazy B.'

'Bit difficult wouldn't you say?'

'Not if you've got the right equipment,' Hamilton spoke triumphantly and bending down picked up a running iron from where it had been thrown into the bushes. 'How very careless.'

'Is that the proof Mr Wallace wants?' Forbes asked, getting off his horse and going up to Ira.

'Proof to us, yeah, maybe. Proof to a court, especially one in Fairmont?' Hamilton shrugged. 'I doubt it. Can't you just see the defence? But, Mr Judge,' he began to mimic a lawyer's voice, 'anyone could have driven those cattle down the hill, anyone could have chosen that spot to brand 'em; why would the Broomes be so stupid as to do that on their own land and then leave the running iron behind? And, Mr Hamilton, did you actually see the Broomes doing this dastardly deed? No, Mr Judge, the Broomes are completely innocent of this charge. And, yeah, us members of the jury agree!'

'I suppose you're right.'

Forbes could hardly believe the evidence of his own eyes. Some of the guys he'd run with in his younger days hadn't been all that smart but even they hadn't been stupid enough to lead a cattle rancher they'd rustled cows from straight to their home base. But he could think of no other explanation than that Hamilton was right and that the Broomes were both stupid and believed they'd never be convicted.

'So what do we do now?'

Hamilton smiled. Forbes really didn't like the man's smile. And said, 'We go pay the Broomes a visit. This may not be good enough for a court of law, but by God it's good enough for me!'

They were halfway across the far meadow approaching a low hill, when from the rocks littering the slope came a puff of smoke. The retort of a rifle was loud on the still air and a heavy bullet smacked into the ground in front of Forbes' horse, kicking up a spray of dust.

The horse whinnied and reared in fright and Forbes, taken by surprise, tumbled backwards out of the saddle, landing with a thump on the ground. Somehow he retained a grip on the reins, his arm almost pulled out of its socket as the horse tried to run away and Forbes dragged hard on the reins to stop it.

Several more shots followed, all of which missed.

'Goddammit!' Hamilton yelled. With a glance at Forbes to see if he was all right, he stabbed spurs into his horse's side and was away off towards the rocks and whoever had fired at them.

Forbes staggered to his feet, wincing as a pain shot up his leg. Otherwise nothing seemed to be hurt.

'OK, OK,' he said, soothing his horse, patting its nose, wishing someone would soothe *him.* His heart was pounding, both with fright and fury. He didn't appreciate being shot at, out of the blue like that! Goddammit—he could have been hurt, killed! He looked towards where Hamilton was urging his horse up the side of the slope. He saw another rider going hell bent for leather for the top, disappearing down the other side, Hamilton in fast pursuit.

Forbes scrambled up into the saddle and gave chase. He caught up with them both at the Broome ranch.

Hamilton had dismounted behind a stack of timber across the open yard from the house. Forbes left his horse by the barn where it couldn't get hit from a stray bullet, and ran across to join the foreman.

'It was the kid,' Hamilton yelled, dragging Forbes down beside him. 'I almost caught up with the little sonofabitch but he was too quick for me and he dived in there.'

Forbes was breathing too heavily to say anything. He drew his revolver, spinning the barrel, checking that all the chambers were full.

Hamilton let off several shots at the house, the bullets thudding into the shutters hastily flung across the windows. 'Come on out you bastards!'

Someone fired out at them, the bullet slapped into the timber, causing chips of wood to fly in all directions.

'Hell!' Forbes ducked down. 'They can hold out in there for as long as they like. We'll never get 'em out.'

'Oh, I don't know,' Hamilton grinned.

'There's usually more 'n one way to skin a goddamned cat.' He nodded towards an untidy group of buildings beyond the barn, one of which was a chicken run.

Forbes followed his gaze and caught a glimpse of a gingham frock before its owner disappeared into the shadows, sending up a clucking of hens.

'Stay here,' Hamilton ordered and ran at a crouch towards the chickens.

'Hey, Ira, don't!' Forbes had no real idea of what was in the man's mind but he didn't think he was going to like it.

'Judith!' A scream of anguish came from someone in the house and automatically Forbes fired in that direction even as another scream came from behind him. The frightened cry of a child. He swung round. Hamilton was coming back, and not alone. Tucked under his arm was a girl of about ten. A cute little girl with brown hair hanging in plaits down her back and tears of fright in her eyes as Hamilton pressed the barrel of his Colt into her forehead.

'For Chrissakes,' Forbes muttered in

disgust. His anger died abruptly. Surely nothing, and especially not five cows, was worth hurting a child for.

'You in the house, come out, or this sweet girl gets her head shot off.'

'Ira! No!'

'Shut up.'

The door to the house was flung back and George Broome stepped out. Beyond him Paul Broome could be seen tugging at his mother's arm to keep her from dashing across to her daughter.

'Let her go, you bastard.'

'Throw your weapons down and come out with your hands up, all of you, then we'll see. Cover 'em, Forbes. Watch out for any tricks.'

'They're unlikely to do anything when you've got hold of the girl,' Forbes said sarcastically.

Left with no choice, the Broome family left the safety of their house. Norah was weeping, another little girl clinging to her skirts, while Broome and Paul stood off to one side, looking both furious and scared.

'It ain't my sister you want, you sonofabitch!' Paul shouted. 'It's me. Come after me if you dare.'

'Paul.' Broome put out a hand, touching his son's arm. 'Don't make it worse.' The man was sweating, eyes darting between Hamilton and Judith, and his wife. It was with a considerable effort that he managed to keep his voice reasonably calm. 'All right, we've done what you asked, now let my daughter go. She's done nothing to you. Don't take your spite out on her.'

'Do as he wants,' Forbes urged.

Hamilton didn't move. It seemed that in that moment everything came to a halt. Forbes was aware of Mrs Broome's crying and of a bird singing over by the barn. And aware of his own heart beating. What would he do if Hamilton kept hold of the girl, or went to shoot her? He couldn't just stand by and let it happen, but would he be quick enough to save her?

Then laughing Hamilton raised his gun and gave the girl a little shove. 'Run to Mummy.'

'Judith! Judith!' Norah Broome screamed

and the girl, sobbing wildly, ran to the safety of her mother's arms. Norah acted quickly, pushing both girls inside and slamming the door shut behind them.

'You bastard,' Broome muttered as soon as he saw they were safe. 'You've no right to come in here, shooting at us and frightening my family.'

'Don't blame me, it's the kid's fault. He was the one shot at us.'

'You were trespassing on our land,' Paul shouted back. 'And after that idiot left that damnfool notice on our door, I had every right to protect us all.'

Hamilton took no notice. Instead grinning he said to Broome, 'We've got the proof to show you're goddamned rustlers.'

'We're not. How many times have we got to tell you that? I don't know what sort of proof you think you've got but...'

'Just this.' The foreman threw the running iron down on the ground. 'We found that in the camp where you've just branded five of Wallace's cattle. Cattle we trailed from the North Pasture to your land.'

'I don't know what the hell you're talking about.'

'It sounds like the sort of thing you'd do yourself to put the blame on us,' Paul said. 'You bastard.'

Hamilton laughed. 'That's what you say. You've been warned often enough, now you've got to face up to the consequences.'

'Damn your warning,' Paul yelled. 'And damn you!' And suddenly he darted forward and lunged at his nearest target—Forbes. His blow landed squarely on Forbes' chin, sending him reeling backwards.

'Dammit,' Forbes muttered. Without really thinking, and using considerably more force than he'd have normally done in the circumstances, he lashed out, catching the young man round the side of the head. Paul went down in the muddy earth of the yard like a suddenly empty sack of potatoes.

'Silly sonofabitch!' Hamilton snarled and gave Paul several vicious kicks in stomach and ribs.

'Stop it!' Broome cried and ran towards his son's attacker.

Hamilton reeled round, raising the gun he still held.

Broome came to a halt.

'Don't!' Forbes stepped forward and knocked Hamilton's gunhand down, just as the man fired. The bullet smacked harmlessly in the mud.

Hamilton turned a furious face towards him. 'What the hell did you do that for?'

'Broome is unarmed unless you hadn't noticed. And the kid is badly hurt.'

Paul was lying on the ground, unconscious, breathing shallowly.

'Serve the bastard right.' And Hamilton kicked him again.

'We've done enough,' Forbes caught hold of Ira's arm, pulling him away. 'Come on, let's leave 'em.'

'Yeah, go on, get outta here,' Broome said, while Norah ran from the house to drop down on her knees in the mud and cradle Paul's head in her lap.

'Mr Wallace won't like this.'

'He'll like cold blooded murder even less. They'll take notice of our warnings now.'

'They'd damn well better.' Hamilton swung back to the Broomes. 'You were lucky here today. We had every right to shoot you. But you don't leave, and soon, and next time you won't get off so lightly.'

Picking up the running iron, Hamilton strode over to his horse. Before following him, Forbes spared a glance for the Broomes. George Broome glared at him but said nothing as he lifted up his injured son and helped by Norah took him into the house.

## NINE

Hamilton also glared at Forbes and then rode away at a full out gallop. Forbes was glad to see him go. Hamilton, in a temper, wasn't someone he wanted to be around. Riding away at a much slower pace, Forbes decided to take a longer route back to the ranch. He had a feeling that even if Mr Wallace drew the line at murder then at least some of his foreman's strongarm tactics would meet with his approval and Forbes wouldn't be all that popular because he had helped put a stop to them.

His journey took him amongst the foothills where he hadn't been before. As he rode along he could hear the sound of a cow bawling in distress. And then as he emerged onto the side of a slope overlooking a grassy meadow, he came to a halt, an amused look on his face.

Below was a muddy waterhole and there stuck in the mud was the cow, pitifully rolling its eyes. And trying to get it out was Mrs Snooty Munroe.

Not that she looked all that snooty now. Her hat was off and some of her hair had come loose. The bottom half of her trousers' legs were covered with mud. She had managed to loop a rope round the cow's neck and was pulling at the animal with no success. Typical of a stupid cow it was pulling in the other direction.

Nearby stood a horse and by it holding

its reins was her son. The boy must have seen Forbes and said something for Mrs Snooty suddenly stopped her tugging and turned to stare up at Forbes.

A look of exasperation came over her face. 'Well don't just sit there grinning at me you damn idiot! Come and help!'

Forbes thought it would serve her right if he just rode away. She really had no call to treat him like she did. But he had no argument with the cow, which then decided to take a scared move backwards. Not expecting it, Alice was jerked off her feet to land face down in the mud.

Forbes couldn't help himself. He burst out laughing.

Alice raised a furious and extremely dirty face towards him. 'It's not funny.'

Still laughing, Forbes jigged his horse down the slope. 'Yeah, it is,' he managed to say and dismounting reached out to help her to her feet.

'If all you can do is laugh you can go away, you stupid idiot!' Alice said angrily and picking up a lump of mud flung it at him.

'Tut, tut, language,' Forbes smirked. 'Just step aside and watch a man do man's work.'

'Oh!' Alice exclaimed and shoved hard at him.

Forbes merely shoved her back so that she almost fell again and took hold of the rope she still had in her hands. He went back to his horse and secured the rope round the saddlehorn. Then walking by the horse, he urged it backwards. The rope stretched taut and as the horse continued to move away, slowly and reluctantly the cow, still bawling piteously, edged forward.

Suddenly the cow was out of the mud. Quickly Forbes freed the rope and yelled 'Look out!' to Alice. The cow shook her head and dashed by them both so that they had to leap out of the way, and it was gone, rope still trailing from its neck.

'Silly, ungrateful thing,' Alice muttered. She turned to Forbes who was trying hard not to laugh at her state. 'I suppose I have to thank you.'

Forbes thought she sounded as silly and ungrateful as the cow. 'I did it for the animal, not you,' he said and because he was so disgusted at her attitude added, 'I suppose it was your own cow and not one of Mr Wallace's.'

It was entirely the wrong thing to say. It started a tirade Forbes was helpless to stop.

'Oh don't worry that cow has my brand on it, I didn't swing a wide loop to get it! Why don't you try and use what little brain you've got, and think? Why should I, or any of my neighbours, have to rustle Mr Wallace's precious cows when I, and they, have cattle of our own? We're not the sodbusters he's trying to make out. We're ranchers. All right on a small scale but ranchers nevertheless and we've all been here a long time.' She poked Forbes in the chest. 'And why should your precious Mr Wallace offer to buy us out when, if we really are rustlers, he could have us arrested and get our land for nothing?'

'He's being generous.'

It was Alice's turn to laugh. 'Please, Mr Forbes, you might be an idiot but don't take me for one!'

'Why don't you sell out to Mr Wallace? I thought his offer was reasonable and it can't be easy for you on your own. Look at today.'

Alice's eyes glittered angrily. 'I can do without your concern, thank you. I'd have managed in the end or got help from someone else. Anyway, what makes you think I'd get the money? I might well not live long enough.'

'What do you mean?'

'For goodness sake, Mr Forbes, use your eyes! Wallace is so determined to prove he can be a rancher, he'd be willing to do anything to achieve what he wants.'

'I don't think so.'

'Don't you? Really?'

Forbes got no chance to say anything more for Billy called out, 'Ma, Ma!' He was pointing along the narrow valley where a rider was approaching.

Alice was startled for a moment, looking at Forbes as if suspecting his being here was some sort of trick, that he'd led Ira Hamilton to her. Then she sighed in relief. 'It's Mr Broome. I wonder what he wants.'

It was Forbes' turn to be apprehensive. He touched the butt of his revolver. Was be going to face more trouble? He didn't want it, he might not be able to avoid it.

'Alice! I've been looking all over for you!' Broome called as he rode up. Then he saw who was with her. 'What the hell is he doing here?'

'He helped me with one of my cows. What's the matter?'

'It's Paul, he's been badly hurt.'

'Oh no! How?'

'He was beaten up by Ira Hamilton and that bastard too.'

'Dammit,' Alice said and flung a hard eyed look at Forbes. 'Picking on boys now are you?'

'It wasn't like that.'

But Alice was already turning back to Broome, ignoring Forbes' protest. 'What can I do?'

'Can you come and help us?'

'Of course.' Alice strode over to her horse. She lifted Billy up into the saddle and mounted behind him. Without a backward glance at Forbes she and Broome rode away, leaving him all alone.

Paul lay unconscious on the bed, a pale sheen of sweat on his forehead, his breathing slow but at least steady. Judith and Rachel hovering at her skirts, Norah Broome was bent over her son doing what little she could for him.

'Oh thank goodness you've come,' she said as Alice was ushered inside by Broome.

'It was all I could do,' Alice replied but, apart from giving the woman some comfort, she didn't really know why she had been summoned. Of course she knew enough to dose coughs and colds. Along with William she had birthed her own baby without any help, and she knew the medicinal qualities of several plants. But she had no more experience of real doctoring than any of the Broomes. To her eyes Paul looked hurt, and badly, and she could suggest nothing else but to take him into the doctor in Fairmont.

'The best thing is to wrap him up and keep him as warm and comfortable as possible. He might have broken a rib or had something hurt inside,' she said while Norah groaned, having her own fears confirmed. 'Oh how could they have done this?'

'To be fair that new man, Forbes, didn't look too happy and he did stop Hamilton shooting me,' Broome said.

Alice wasn't prepared to be so fair minded. 'He's with them isn't he? I don't like what's happening.'

'Nor do I. We didn't take those cows or drive them onto our land or leave a running iron behind. I haven't got a running iron. So who did do all that?' Broome answered his own question. 'I think Hamilton did it himself so as to be able to lay the blame on us and have an excuse to become violent and throw us out. It would be easy for an experienced hand like him to drive five or six cows all that way on his own. Then scatter them while he built a fire and pretended that some branding had taken place. And later bring along this new man as a witness, if he wasn't in on it all along. I bet if the running iron doesn't prove enough for a court of law then he'll conveniently find the cattle still with the Rocking W brand on 'em on our land.'

Alice frowned. 'It sounds possible. Do you think Wallace put him up to it?'

'You know very well, Alice, that it wouldn't be the first time something was done behind Wallace's back so he could conveniently say he knows nothing about it.'

'Paul is who matters now,' Norah interrupted. 'We must take him into town.'

Broome laid a hand on his wife's arm. 'It's too late to set out today. It'll be getting dark soon. We'll leave first thing tomorrow. Will you come with us, Alice?'

'Of course. I'll meet you on the road at, what, seven o'clock? You won't let this make any difference will you?'

Broome and Norah looked at one another.

'Please.'

'We'll have to wait and see.'

Wallace listened eagerly to what Hamilton had to tell him. 'Good news at last! It was a pity you didn't have time to actually follow the trail some more and discover my five missing cows.'

'Even if we had done, the cows would have been in the middle of a much larger herd with the brand already changed. Unless of course Forbes and me got there too quickly for 'em and scared 'em away before they could use the running iron.'

'Still that running iron should be enough for a court of law.'

'But, sir, I thought you said going to the law wouldn't do any good.'

'The local law, that's true. But with this I reckon I've got a good enough case to ask, no demand, that the County Sheriff in Laramie send a judge out here to hear the case. The Broomes are sure to be convicted.'

Hamilton hid an angry sigh. He didn't understand his boss. Sometimes he seemed perfectly willing for Ira to use violence; other times he wanted to use the law. He'd soon find he couldn't have it both ways, not out here. And hadn't he realized by now that everyone was on the side of the sodbusters? If the trial was held in Fairmont, no matter what the evidence, nor who the judge, it was doubtful the Broomes would be found guilty. The best thing would be for the trial to be held in Laramie, or, better still, if the Broomes never got to trial at all.

'I shall go into Fairmont tomorrow. I have a few business matters to attend to, and I'll see the Marshal at the same time and demand that he do something about this.'

## TEN

From the cafe window, Laura Reynolds saw the two buckboards being driven slowly along towards Main Street. Mr Broome drove the first one, with the two girls on the seat beside him and Mrs Broome in the back. Where was Paul? Something must have happened! Heart bumping with fright, Laura ran out into the street.

'What's wrong?' she cried and then, seeing Paul lying beside his mother, screeched in alarm.

'Come with me, Laura,' Alice called. 'We're taking Paul to the doctor's. I'll tell you what happened on the way.'

Doctor Terry lived and worked in a large two storied house on the edge of town. As they came to a halt outside, the doctor, senses tuned to when his services were needed, came to the door.

'It's my son,' Broome said. 'He's been beaten up.'

'Bring him in.'

'Billy, you play in the garden with Rachel and Judith. And be good all of you.' Alice took hold of Laura's cold hand.

Helped by Norah, Broome carried Paul into the house and down to the room at the back where the doctor saw to his more seriously ill patients. He was laid on the bed and Doctor Terry ushered them all out.

'I'll be as quick as I can,' he promised. All the same it seemed an awfully long time before he came out.

'Is he going to be all right? Oh please let him be!' Laura cried.

Doctor Terry smiled. 'Paul will be fine. He's badly bruised and will probably have a number of aches and pains for a while but luckily there's nothing broken. A rest for a few days and he'll be as good as new.'

'Thank God!' Norah collapsed against her husband's shoulder in relief.

'He's awake. You can all go in and see him.'

This was a family matter and Alice didn't want to intrude. She touched Broome's arm. 'Can you look after Billy for a while? I've got some things to do. Casey needs to know about this.'

Broome nodded. 'Yeah. Maybe Wallace has allowed his men to go too far this time.'

'I'm glad Paul is going to be all right. I'll see you later.' Alice put on her old hat

116

and hurried out. Now to take the fight to her enemy.

While Richard Wallace was in Fairmont he did some business at the bank, which involved drawing out more of his father's cash, and decided that later on he'd visit the best brothel. In Wallace's mind "best" wasn't the term he would use, but Madame Clara's was the most expensive cathouse in town and her girls were reasonably young and pretty. In between he paid a visit on Marshal Patterson.

Now, a bored look on his handsome face, he stared at the lawman and tried not to lose his temper. Really the gall of these small town citizens. Give them a bit of power and they thought themselves so important. As far as Wallace was concerned, Fairmont was a speck on the plains and its town marshal a complete nobody.

And here he was daring to argue. 'I just can't believe that the Broomes are rustlers,' Patterson repeated.

'I don't care what you believe or what

you don't! My foreman found proof on their land. And I want you to get in touch with the law in Laramie and ask that a judge come out here to conduct a trial. Or is that too much for your limited capabilities?' Wallace used the tone that back East he'd used on the servants. It was calculated to insult. 'If not then I shall see to it that the Broomes are taken to Laramie and the trial held there. I think you'd know the outcome then?'

Patterson did. The law and the citizens of Laramie were controlled by the large ranchers. The Broomes would not only be found guilty they'd be punished as harshly as possible. There was no way out of this. Wallace had the law, if not the right, on his side.

Wallace banged his hands down on the man's desk. 'Now, when can the judge be here?'

'It depends. Could be a couple of weeks, could be longer.'

'Well, try to make it as soon as possible. Meanwhile I want an eye kept on the Broomes and all the others like them and

I don't want excuses such as you're just town marshal. I want something done. Understand?'

'Yes, Sir. I thought you were doing something yourself.'

'What exactly does that mean?'

'The man, Forbes, you've recently employed.'

'What about him?'

'What exactly is his role?'

'He's a cowhand, of course.'

'Pardon me, Mr Wallace, but he neither looks nor behaves like an experienced cowhand.'

An annoyed tone in his voice, Wallace said, 'Well that's what he is, Marshal. What other kind of man would I employ? Now, if there's nothing more, I'm very busy.'

'No, there's nothing more.' Patterson watched the man go. There were times when he thought of giving up as marshal and this surely was one of them.

Casey Chapman also knew that Richard Wallace was in town. He saw him go into the marshal's office and then watched as the man headed for the hotel and the only restaurant in town; Reynolds' cafe obviously not being good enough. When Wallace first arrived in Fairmont, Chapman had presented himself out at the ranch and secured an interview with him. It had been the first and only report on Wallace that showed the rancher in a good light. Before long Chapman started to write articles about him that weren't to the man's liking. After that, naturally, Wallace had refused to see him and had had him thrown off the Rocking W.

But maybe Chapman could get a few words from him while he was here.

Gathering up notepad and pencil, Chapman put on his bowler hat and thick jacket and hurried down to the hotel. By the time he got there Wallace had started on the soup course. He was also reading a piece of paper and didn't notice the editor until he'd sat down opposite him.

'What the hell are you doing here?' Wallace demanded angrily, spluttering his soup a bit, so that it spilt down the front of his tie.

'Wondered if you might like to say a few words for *The Enquirer*, Mr Wallace.'

'No, I wouldn't! How dare you disturb me like this! I'll have you thrown out of here!'

'Oh, I don't think so. It's not like at your ranch, you know, people in town aren't willing to kowtow to you.'

And when Wallace looked round, he saw the truth of this. The head waiter and the two waitresses, who just a few moments before had been bustling round the dining room, had somehow disappeared. The other diners resolutely had their heads down and were taking no notice.

'Maybe you'd like to say something about why your men beat up young Paul Broome, so that he's even now fighting for his life over at the doctor's?'

Wallace said a very rude word in reply.

'Can I quote you on that? I'm sure my readers would like to read about your concern.'

'How dare you speak to me like this! I

won't answer your questions. I don't know what you're talking about.' There was a sulky boyish look on Wallace's face. 'All I've done I've done fairly.'

'Including putting a notice on the Broomes' door threatening them with a lynching because of their rustling activities when they aren't rustlers, any more than I am. They don't need to be, they have their own cattle.'

'Isn't it by rustling that these sodbusters get their cattle in the first place?'

'Come off it,' Chapman lost his own temper. 'The Broomes are an honest family. Or at least they were until you came out here with your lies.'

'I'm fed up with you and the other sanctimonious citizens taking the side of the sodbusters. You only hate me because I'm rich and have some pretensions of civilisation.'

Chapman laughed, causing Wallace to flinch angrily. No one laughed at him.

'If you remember aright, Wallace, when you first came here, everyone was willing to welcome you. You'd been the talk of the place for weeks before you arrived. Several people went out to your ranch offering help in getting you set up.'

'Because of my money.'

'I admit it was hoped you'd have plenty to spend. But not only that. They hoped also that you'd be able to bring some good manners to the place. Instead they soon found out you had no manners. You were rude, you looked down on everyone, you wanted your own way. No wonder people don't like you and think you're foolish. Mr Wallace, you blew it!' And Casey stood up and walked away.

Wallace watched him go. He turned back to his soup and wasn't pleased to notice that the hand holding the spoon shook slightly. 'This is cold now,' he yelled at the waiter who had re-appeared. 'Get me some more.'

'Yes, sir.'

Was this man mocking him as that damn editor had said people were? How dare he? No one laughed at him, no one spoke to him like that. Chapman had bitten off more than he could chew if he thought he could get away with that, and so had the whole damn town! Hamilton was right—force was all these people understood and that being the case he'd damn well give it to them!

Wallace was still fuming when he got back home. Pacing backwards and forwards across the rug in front of the fireplace, he denounced Fairmont, its citizens, in particular Casey Chapman, and Alice Munroe; while Hamilton looked on, hoping that, at last, here was the chance to commit mayhem.

'I don't know who the hell they all think they are.' Wallace flung the latest edition of *The Enquirer* into the grate and flung himself behind the oak desk. He leant forward and eyed Hamilton. 'Chapman writes twaddle about me and everyone else believes it. No one likes me, do they? Why not? What have I ever done to them?' He looked and sounded like a petulant schoolboy.

'Chapman and that Mrs Munroe are both thorns in my side. It would solve an awful lot of my problems if one was to accept my generous offer for her ranch and the other was to give up writing scurrilous editorials about me. I really won't tolerate these slurs on my good name, not any more.'

Hamilton smirked. He knew only too well that his boss was giving his silent permission for him to do whatever was necessary to make Mrs Munroe quit her ranch and to stop Chapman running the newspaper. One or other, or both of them, must have upset him when he was in town. It didn't really matter. All that mattered was that his boss was at last seeing sense.

The foreman went quickly from the study to the bunkhouse. 'Mr Wallace wants us all to go into town tomorrow, buy some supplies, see what's happening.'

'All of us?' Forbes asked.

'That's right. He thinks there could be trouble and he wants us to be ready for it. You game, Forbes, or do you want to stay behind?'

'Of course I'll come, I ain't scared,'

Forbes said angrily. He was aware of the smile on Hamilton's face and feared there was something more behind this trip than the foreman was letting on.

## ELEVEN

'Come on, drink up,' Hamilton ordered, downing the rest of his own beer. 'We've got to go.'

'Where?' Forbes asked.

He had wondered why Hamilton suggested going into The Bull's Head for a drink or two before starting out on Richard Wallace's business. Now he thought that maybe it had something to do with getting them all drunk first, although it would take more than a couple of whiskies to get Forbes drunk. Certainly though Del and Burt had glints of excitement in their eyes that weren't usually there.

Forbes was beginning to think that he'd been wrong about the pair of them. Maybe they weren't ordinary cowhands after all or maybe it was just that following the hard and lonely work out on the ranch they wanted to kick ass when they came to town. Whatever the truth, at the moment, they looked quite prepared to get involved in any mischief Hamilton might suggest.

'We're going to pay a visit on Mr Casey Chapman,' Hamilton explained. 'Mr Wallace is fed up with him taking the side of the sodbusters. We ain't going to let him do it any more.'

Del nudged Burt and the two young men stood up.

'Coming, Forbes?'

'Yeah, OK.' Reluctantly Forbes followed them out of the saloon and towards the newspaper office.

Leaving Billy with Mrs McGee, Alice hurried along to Doctor Terry's. The Broomes had stayed with her at the boarding house and they and Casey Chapman had talked long into the night about the situation and what they could do about it. Marshal Patterson had also been by to warn the Broomes that Wallace was forcing him to send for the judge from Laramie and that he really ought to put out a warrant for their arrest. Casey had promised to do what he could but it all seemed a bit forlorn. And Alice knew she would be Wallace's next target.

The Broomes had left earlier that morning for the doctor's and were now sitting in the bedroom with their son. Laura was with them too, looking as if she'd been up crying half the night.

'I've just come to see how Paul is,' Alice said. 'Then I'm going to see Casey, buy some supplies and go home.'

'Doc says Paul's doing well. He can probably go home in a couple of days' time,' Broome replied. 'We're going to leave him in Laura's capable hands,' he smiled across at the girl, 'and go home ourselves, get on with the work.'

'I'm sure Laura will look after Paul splendidly.'

The young girl smiled. 'I'll do my best. Later on today we're moving him over to the spare room at the cafe.'

As Alice went to go, Broome accompanied her to the door. 'Alice, be careful, I've heard Hamilton is in town.'

Alice didn't like the way her heart missed a frightened beat. 'I will. You too, Mr Broome.'

Casey Chapman sat at his desk, tapping the quill pen against his teeth and thinking about his next editorial. The rest of the paper was ready—the usual snippets about births, deaths, marriages and the price of cows back East. He wanted to write something explosive about Mr Richard Wallace and his latest activities. Something to make the rancher understand that he couldn't allow his men to ride roughshod over everyone and expect to get away with it.

His reverie was broken as the door was flung open and four men rushed in.

'Jesus Christ!' Chapman exclaimed, jumping to his feet with shock, tipping the chair back. Seeing Ira Hamilton his heart flipped over with fear. He thought about reaching for the revolver he kept in the desk drawer but realized he would stand no chance against four of them and might just give them the excuse to shoot him. Hoping his voice didn't sound as shaky as he felt, he said, 'What the hell do you want here?'

'Mr Wallace doesn't like the goddamned lies you've been spreading about him,' Hamilton snarled. 'Especially these.' And he threw the latest copy of *The Enquirer* at Chapman.

'It's not lies.'

'Oh, yeah, it is.' And Hamilton punched the newspaperman hard on the side of his cheek, knocking him backwards against the wall.

Del then gave him a violent push. Chapman fell to the floor, his glasses going askew and as he made a grab for them, they fell off. Chapman fumbled for them but Hamilton was quicker, pounding his foot down on the spectacles, grinding them to bits.

'Destroy his machine!' Burt yelled.

'No!' Chapman screamed but as he tried to struggle to his feet, Hamilton kicked his legs out from under him and he went down again.

At the same time Del and Burt began to rock the printing press backwards and forwards. And Hamilton knocked a tray over, scattering the pieces of type, stamping on them.

Forbes looked on, wondering what to do. Bullying and wanton destruction had never been his style, although both Mr Wallace and Hamilton had obviously thought differently. And he wasn't drunk enough, like Del and Burt, to pretend that it was. He was saved from having to decide on anything by the office door opening.

'Casey,' Alice Munroe said and then seeing what was happening, she cried, 'Casey' again. 'Stop that!' she shouted, dashing at Hamilton, trying to knock him over.

Hamilton grabbed at her and shoved her away, towards Forbes. 'Get her outta here!'

131

'Don't touch me!' she said and slapped Forbes hard round the face.

'Ow!' he exclaimed and caught hold of her round the waist, lifting her off her feet. 'Come with me.'

'Let me go, you bastard!' she screamed, beginning to struggle.

Forbes had no choice but to manhandle her. He was scared that if she stayed, Hamilton would hurt her and he wanted her out of the way. But Alice obviously didn't see it the same way and didn't make it easy. She fought him hard, squirming and kicking, arms flailing. As he carried her to the door, he somehow got it open, while she tried to punch him. They struggled outside and Forbes dragged her round to the back of the newspaper office where they couldn't be seen by curious passersby. He put her down and for a moment they stood facing one another, Forbes holding Alice's arms, panting with effort.

Alice kicked him hard on the shin.

'Don't!' Forbes winced with pain. 'I ain't never hit a woman...'

'You surprise me.'

'...but that don't mean I can't start now.'

'Oh you think you're so brave don't you?' Alice said angrily. 'Four men picking on one. Just like you and that thug Hamilton picked on Paul.'

'Paul shot at me and then punched me first.'

'So that makes it all right does it? He's a boy! He was trying to defend his home and family but that doesn't mean anything to you does it? All you're concerned about is Wallace's money. You'd do anything for that. You're a real bastard.'

'You keep making what you think of me very clear.'

'Oh be quiet.' Alice curled her lip in disgust.

She tried to push by him and he caught her arm. 'Where are you going?'

'In to see Casey.'

'Not yet. They'll hurt you if you do.'

'And you won't?' Alice deliberately rubbed her arm where Forbes had held her roughly.

'Not unless I have to.'

'It's all about what Casey writes isn't it? Your precious Mr Wallace doesn't like the truth.'

'According to Hamilton it's lies.'

'And what do you think?'

Forbes shrugged. 'I don't know. I can't read.'

'Why does that come as no surprise? Well, Mr Forbes, for your information Casey is right. He's also very brave. Do you think that whatever your cronies are doing will make any difference to Casey, or to me? Your Mr Wallace has hurt me badly enough already. He can't hurt me any more. Now, Mr Forbes, I'm going in there and if you want to stop me you'll have to do so by force.' And shoving him aside, she stalked away, hands clenched in fists by her sides as if she longed to hit someone.

Forbes followed her and as they got to the front of the building, the others came out. Forbes got a glimpse of the inside of the office; the printing press was lying on its side, some of it broken, the desk was on its back, legs in the air, and ink, type and torn paper lay scattered across the floor. Casey Chapman lay in the middle of it all, face cut and bruised, eyes closed.

'Casey!' Alice wailed and rushed inside to him.

'Come on, Forbes,' Ira Hamilton said, a pleased look on his face, while Del and Burt giggled helplessly together. 'Let's go back to the saloon! Celebrate!'

Forbes cast one look back at Alice. He wasn't at all sure about this but as some of the townsfolk began to gather to see what was going on, there were angry murmurs against the ranchhands. Not wanting to be left alone in the middle of a possibly hostile crowd, he went with Hamilton.

'Casey! Casey!' Alice bent over the editor.

Blearily he opened his eyes, saw her and smiled, but then moaned and closed his eyes again, wincing.

'Stay where you are. I'll get Doctor Terry.'

135

'No, I can walk. If you help me.' Chapman reached up an arm, putting it round her shoulders. 'I can't see properly. My glasses?'

'There's nothing left of them,' Alice told him. She held him tightly, as he limped towards the door. There more willing hands reached out and Chapman was helped down the road.

Again Doctor Terry came to the door. 'Well, well, Alice, you are bringing me a lot of patients these days.'

'You should have seen what the sons-ofbitches have done to his office,' Mr Reynolds said. 'It's completely destroyed. Don't you worry, Casey, the town won't let 'em get away with this. We'll start up a collection, or something.'

'Yeah, that's right,' other voices took up the cry.

'Oh, Casey,' Alice said with tears in her eyes as she handed him over to the doctor's care. Then she turned back to the crowd. 'I'm going to see the Marshal. Who's coming with me?'

'I will,' Reynolds replied.

'But Marshal you must do something!' Alice put her hands on the man's scarred desk and leaned forward, her body quivering with indignation. 'You must!'

'Alice, dear, I'm town marshal and...'

'And this happened in the town! You can't ignore it.'

'But the men who did it come from out of town. I can't arrest them.'

'I don't see why not,' Reynolds put in. 'Alice's right. This is the first time the bastards have done anything like this in Fairmont. Surely that gives you the excuse to arrest 'em.'

Patterson ran a hand over his balding head. 'It's not that easy.' Then he decided to admit the truth. 'There are four of them, one of me. The Town Council don't pay me enough to hire any deputies. I'm all right dealing with collecting taxes, locking up the odd drunk and even keeping the redlight district in order. I ain't cut out to go up against gunmen. I'm not a gunfighter and never have been. They'd shoot me down before I had a chance.'

'Oh, Fred,' Alice sighed.

'I'm real sorry, Alice,' Patterson said sadly and refused to look at her.

'Hey look!' Del said and the other three followed his gaze out of the saloon's window.

Across the road Alice Munroe, her little boy sitting beside her, was driving out of town. In the back of the buckboard were several sacks of supplies.

'She's a real snooty bitch!' Hamilton said, his face flushed and excited with the drink he'd consumed. 'What say we teach her a lesson?'

'Yeah!' Del and Burt said together.

Forbes' protest of 'Hey now, wait a minute,' was lost as the others pushed their chairs back and stood up. Heart heavy, he went with them as they hurried down to the livery stable where they'd left their horses.

A few angry glances were cast their way but so far no one had called them out for what they'd done to Casey Chapman.

Later on when meetings were held in saloons and drink bolstered bravery it might be different. Forbes didn't want to go with Hamilton, neither did he want to brazen it out in town all by himself. So he rode amongst the other three men as they galloped out of town but he didn't join in their whoops of excitement.

'Ma?'

'It's OK Billy.' Alice glanced over her shoulder. 'I know they're coming.' She had been aware of the riders pursuing her since they'd first appeared on the horizon. And she knew who they were. She eased the shotgun onto her knees and whipped the horse up into a gallop.

'We'll never outrun 'em, Ma.'

Billy was right and within moments the four men were all round her and the buckboard, leaving her no choice but to pull the horse to a halt.

'What do you want?' she cried out. 'Leave me alone.' She raised the shotgun but the one called Del rode up by her and despite Billy's cry of alarm, moved too swiftly for Alice. He caught hold

139

of the gun, dragging it out of Alice's grasp and throwing it on the ground. Alice stood up and Del put his arm round her, pulling her off the wagon seat and giving her a push that sent her sprawling.

'Ma! Ma!' Billy screamed and he jumped down running to his mother.

'I'm all right,' Alice told him, getting to her feet.

Forbes sat on his horse, watching the others ride round and round the buckboard, sending up a whirl of dust, while Alice and her son clung to one another, Billy beginning to cry.

Del and Burt jumped off their horses and ran up to the buckboard, Laughing they started to pick up the bags of supplies and throw them on the ground. Flour spilled over the scrubby grass and tins scattered everywhere.

Forbes rode over to Hamilton. 'Ain't you going to stop them? This has gone far enough.'

'She deserves all she's getting.' Hamilton had a gleam in his eyes. It wasn't just of excitement, it was of something mean. 'Maybe she should get even more.'

'What do you mean?'

'What the hell do you think? She's a good looking woman or hadn't you noticed?' Hamilton slowly got off his horse. He strolled over to the buckboard. 'Leave that now,' he said to Del and Burt. They stopped what they doing and, grinning, flanked their foreman.

Hamilton pushed Billy away so that he fell. 'Come here,' he said to Alice and caught hold of her arm.

'Stop it!' she said, her voice shrill with fright. 'Please.'

It was getting ugly and Forbes was scared it was going to get even uglier. Del and Burt were drunk and capable of anything and Hamilton was a vicious thug, willing to lead them on. All Alice's pleading would do no good, it would probably make it worse.

'Leave her alone,' Forbes found himself saying. As the three men swung round towards him, he pulled out his gun and pointed it directly at Hamilton's head.

# TWELVE

Hamilton laughed but there was no mirth in the sound. 'Don't be so goddamned stupid, Forbes.'

'I mean it. Get away from her, all of you. I don't hold with threatening women and kids, nor with what you had in mind, Ira.'

With all three men's attention on Forbes, Billy ran over to pick up his mother's shotgun. Del's hand moved towards his gun. Forbes caught sight of the movement and at the same time Alice called out a warning.

'Don't do that!'

Del glared at Forbes. 'I'll get you for this.'

'You'll have to wait in line,' Hamilton said with a snarl.

Meanwhile Alice took the gun from her son and said, 'You ought to do as Mr

Forbes says. Even if he doesn't shoot you, I will.'

'She means it,' Burt swallowed nervously, because it was his chest at which Alice was aiming the gun. He'd suddenly sobered up and looked thoroughly ashamed of himself. 'Shall we go?'

For a moment Hamilton hesitated. He had a feeling neither Forbes nor Alice was bluffing. While he could beat either of them in any gunfight, he couldn't beat both of them, at least not without back up, nor with their guns already out. And while Del might stand by him, Burt was no longer enjoying this and wanted only to get away.

'There'll be another chance,' he said and swaggered back to his horse. 'You're a goddamned fool, Forbes,' he added. 'You had a good job and more money than you're ever likely to earn again. You've thrown it all away on some bitch who normally wouldn't even acknowledge you in the street.'

'There are some things worth more than money.'

'Oh my, what high principles all of a sudden! Well I hope you think you're right in a few days' time. Meanwhile just watch out or you could find yourself in real danger one dark night.'

'Get outta here before you're the one in danger.'

The three men spurred their horses into a gallop. As the sound of the hoofbeats died away in the distance, Forbes and Alice looked at one another. Slowly she lowered the shotgun and equally slowly he reholstered his gun.

'Why did you help me?'

Forbes shrugged. 'I don't know. I couldn't stand by and let you be hurt.'

Alice went round to the back of the buckboard and began picking up some of the spilled supplies. Billy kept by her side, tears still pricking at his eyes. 'You won't be very popular back at the Rocking W. Mr Richard Wallace won't like you siding with a sodbuster.'

'I thought you weren't a sodbuster.' Forbes got off his horse and went to help her. The flour was beyond salvation but most of the canned goods were intact. 'I ain't scared of Mr Wallace. He's all bluster.'

'What about Hamilton?'

'Yeah, I guess I am scared of him,' he was honest enough to admit. 'And so should you be.'

'I can look after myself.'

'Sure you can. Anyway I shan't be going back to the ranch.'

'So what will you do?'

'First of all I'm going to ride back to your place with you, make sure the bastards ain't waiting in ambush up ahead. Then, well, I don't rightly know. Probably move on. Find something some place else that's more to my taste than all this.' Forbes wished he'd never heard of Richard Wallace or his ranch; things were much easier before. He'd had to take too many decisions lately.

'You don't have to come with me. We'll be all right. I'm quite used to fending for myself.'

'There's no need to be so prickly, Mrs Munroe. Why not accept the help that's

145

freely offered?'

Alice went red and turned quickly away, so that Forbes wouldn't see the tears that suddenly appeared in her eyes. She had been very scared, certain that the men were going to hurt her, or even worse hurt Billy. This man, Forbes, had gone out on a limb for her and instead of thanking him she had retreated into the shell she put round herself and carried on being her usual ungracious self.

'All right,' she mumbled.

'So Mr Forbes has a conscience has he?' Richard Wallace looked at his foreman through narrowed eyes, his normally handsome face ugly with anger. 'Couldn't it have been prevented?'

'I don't see how,' Hamilton replied. 'I never trusted Forbes from the beginning, if you remember? I thought it was a mistake all along to hire him.' He shrugged. 'I'm glad to be rid of him.' He thought Wallace was only worrying about the money he'd spent on Forbes, nothing else.

'Well, I don't suppose it matters much

anyway. Forbes won't stay around long. He knows he won't get much of a welcome in Fairmont and he's the type to turn tail and run at the first sign of discomfort.'

'He won't cause me any difficulty. He tries, I can handle him.'

'Like you handled Chapman, I hope?'

'Yeah, it'll take some time and a helluva lot of money to get his newspaper started up again.' Hamilton's eyes sparkled with remembrance at all the destruction they'd caused in the newspaper office. 'That is, if Chapman is anxious to risk another beating.'

Wallace smiled. 'I don't suppose he will be. I know his type as well. Another one of these idiots who thinks a pen is mightier than the sword and then gets a terrible jolt when they find out differently. But,' the rancher turned serious, 'Alice Munroe is quite another matter. What on earth put it in your heads to chase and threaten her?'

'I thought you wanted her dealt with.'

'Not like that.' Wallace thumped his hands on the desk. 'I credited you with more sense. The townsfolk will be angry enough at what was done to Chapman, they'll be up in arms if they learn that Mrs Munroe was almost raped, even if they don't believe she's a lady.'

'We didn't touch her,' Hamilton said sulkily.

'Only because Forbes stopped you. You were fools! Oh don't get me wrong. I couldn't care less whether you raped her or not. If you had, it might have done the trick and made her leave. What I am concerned about is what the town will make of it. You have to be careful with the way you handle women.'

'I'm sorry.'

'Oh well, the damage is done I suppose. Perhaps,' Wallace stroked his beard thoughtfully, 'I'd better ride out there tomorrow and make conciliatory noises. You can come with me and apologize as well. Perhaps she'll believe that you were all so drunk you couldn't help yourselves and that you're now sorry. And maybe she'll be foolish enough to forgive you and agree to say nothing.'

'And if she ain't?'

'Then, Ira, we'll have to think of something else.'

Forbes and Alice said nothing further on the ride back to the ranch. Forbes kept his eyes open for any sign of Hamilton and the others but it seemed they'd decided to go back to the Rocking W. When they got into the yard he dismounted and started to unload the supplies.

'You don't have to do that,' Alice said. 'I can manage.'

Forbes ignored her, thinking that was the best way to treat her. He lifted up the bag of supplies and said, 'Show me where you want these put.' She might insist on being ungracious, it didn't mean he had to be as well.

Inside, the house was shabby but clean, full of homemade furniture, that was sturdy and well crafted. In one corner of the main room stood a table, covered with a bright cloth, and four ladder backed chairs. A couple of comfortable chairs with scatter cushions on them were grouped round a rug in front of the fireplace. Several vases contained flowers. By a wooden staircase was the door to the kitchen. This was a tiny room, dominated by a wood-burning stove, with gleaming copper pots and pans on wooden shelves.

'Would you like a cup of coffee?' Alice asked, after she and Forbes had stacked the supplies away.

'Wouldn't say no.'

'And there's some beefpie left from yesterday.'

'Fine.'

This short burst of speech was followed by an awkward silence. Alice turned away to light the stove leaving Forbes feeling that the room was much too small for the two of them.

Then abruptly Alice swung round and much to the surprise of them both, said, 'Mr Forbes, would you stay and help me on the ranch?'

And to the surprise of himself and Alice, Forbes said, 'All right, yeah, I will.'

'I can't pay you much,' Alice went on in a rush, as if regretting both her impulsive offer and his acceptance of it. 'I mean, really, at the moment I can't pay you anything.'

'Bed and board will do,' Forbes said. And then went red, hoping that by bed, she didn't think he meant sharing her's.

'And there's a lot of work to do.'

'I can see that for myself.'

'And you might not be accepted by my neighbours, and...'

'Mrs Munroe,' Forbes interrupted, 'do you want me here or not? You were the one asked me but if you've changed your mind then I'll go.'

'No, I want you to stay.'

'Then, ma'am, I will.'

Forbes thought he'd probably made the right choice—although why he'd made it remained a mystery—when he ate the supper she put in front of him. It was both good and plentiful. And it made a change to be sitting at a table with a cloth on it and eating with good cutlery, the room lit by the pale light of an oil lamp.

At the same time he wondered if it really was the right choice. Mrs Snooty was an uppity woman who didn't appeal to him in the slightest. And here he was working for her! He'd be taking orders from her. And as for her son, Billy, well what did he know about kids? And Billy was an odd boy, who didn't behave like most kids of his age. He never seemed to laugh or smile. He rarely spoke. And he spent most of the meal looking at Forbes as if he was a different species.

And if that was the 'board' part of his employment, what about the 'bed'?

Nothing had been said about that.

Where exactly was he going to sleep? Apart from his mother, Forbes had rarely been around any decent women. His female acquaintances consisted of prostitutes. He knew where he stood with whores. You paid them, or their pimp, they took you back to their room, and after some pawing and panting you went away satisfied.

Decent women, and despite her swearing and outlandish dress, that was the category into which Mrs Munroe obviously came, were there to be respected. They didn't like pawing and panting, especially if they weren't married, and sometimes not even then. But Mrs Munroe was a widow so did that make any difference? She was also apparently fooling around with Casey Chapman—but did that mean she'd be willing to fool around with anyone else?

Despite the fact that Mrs Munroe wasn't his type, Forbes couldn't help but be hopeful that perhaps she wasn't quite as decent as he thought and that he might end up in bed with her; it had after all been some time since he'd enjoyed a woman's favours and here he was in close proximity to one, actually in her house, sitting at her table. But dare he make the first move? When to do so might mean the shotgun stuck in his belly and when he wouldn't put it past Mrs Munroe to pull the trigger?

Alice solved the problem for him. Once they'd finished supper and Billy had gone to do the washing up, she went upstairs, returning with a pillow and a couple of blankets.

'You can sleep in the barn, Mr Forbes, it's quite comfortable. Do you mind? There was never any need to build a bunkhouse.'

'I've slept in worse places, ma'am.' Disappointed Forbes took the bedclothes from her and trundled outside and across to the barn. As he got there, the light in the house went out.

If Forbes had doubts about accepting the job, Alice was definitely having doubts about offering it to him. As she lay in bed, she asked herself again why she had done so.

She knew nothing about him, except that he was a drunk and had ridden for her enemy, Mr Wallace, and had been quite willing to beat up young Paul and poor Casey. Just because he had saved her from being raped didn't mean he had reformed any of his other bad ways. And now here she was alone with him, having invited him into her house.

Well, she and the ranch wanted a saviour but as she fell asleep, Alice couldn't help but think that Forbes was a most unlikely knight in shining armour.

# THIRTEEN

'Ow!' For the third time that morning Forbes hit his thumb rather than the nail with the hammer. He resisted, somehow, both doing a dance of pain and swearing, because not far away Billy sat watching him. Swearing would be a bad influence on the boy, because the language Forbes had in mind was much worse than the boy's mother used, and dancing around hollering would make the boy think Forbes was even more of a fool than he clearly considered him already. In fact, Forbes wished wholeheartedly that the kid would take himself off and go and play elsewhere. His unspeaking, unblinking presence was getting on Forbes' nerves. He wanted to be left to get on with the work in his own way; in other words to do as little as possible.

Over breakfast, Forbes had asked Alice

what she wanted done first. 'I'd better stay near to the house for a day or two,' he'd added, 'just in case Hamilton decides to pay a call and carry on where he left off.'

'OK,' Alice nodded in reply. 'There's so much needs doing it doesn't really matter where you start.'

'What about the barn? I noticed last night there were several gaps which need plugging up. They made it so cold, it almost prevented me going to sleep.'

If Forbes expected any sort of sympathy, he didn't get it. 'There are nails and a hammer in the shack outside the kitchen. You'll need to cut some wood.'

'What will you be doing, ma'am?'

'It's washday, Mr Forbes. Please feel free to put out anything you need washing.'

Was that a hint that he smelt? He probably did, he admitted to himself, and taking her at her word, gave her his dirty shirt and socks. Washday, he knew, was something most women dreaded and he was glad to be working on the other side of the barn where he couldn't get involved.

Not so good was the fact that Billy had trailed after him, keeping his distance, and had settled down to play in the dirt nearby, which was where he stayed.

Along about mid afternoon Forbes heard riders approach. He'd been working hard most of the time, which was most unusual for him, and glad of any excuse to break off, he put down hammer and nails and went to the corner of the barn. Richard Wallace and Ira Hamilton had come to a halt by the line of washing Alice was hanging out. And they didn't look any too friendly. Wallace was talking and gesticulating, while Hamilton sat silently on his horse, his expression sullen.

'Stay here outta sight,' Forbes warned Billy and walked out into the open.

As he saw him, Hamilton's mouth twisted into an ugly sneer and he said something to Wallace, who also turned in Forbes' direction.

'Well, well,' Hamilton said as Forbes came up to Alice. 'It ain't taken you long to get your feet under the table.'

'Watch your mouth, Ira, it ain't like that at all.'

'Oh no? Mr Wallace's money obviously wasn't as good as moving in on a widow woman.'

'Shut up with your filthy insinuations,' Alice snapped.

'Be quiet,' Wallace said to his foreman in a warning tone. 'I'm quite sure there's nothing untoward in this relationship. They are employer and employee. Mrs Munroe has far too much good taste to take up with someone like Forbes. Or at least I hope she has. The good citizens of Fairmont already look at her somewhat askance. I wouldn't like to think what they'd make of an indelicate situation out here. At the least they'd take her son away from her. More probably they'd drive her away.'

'There ain't anything improper in me being out here as a hired hand,' Forbes said angrily. 'And don't try to make out there is.'

'You a hired hand?' Hamilton laughed. 'You don't know one end of a goddamned cow from another. You're here for one reason only and that's to have your way with her.'

'You'd better go,' Forbes said. 'Before you say something we'll all regret.'

Wallace touched the brim of his hat. 'There's clearly no point in trying to talk sense to either of you. We'll just have to see what other people make of this.'

'What did they want?' Forbes asked when they'd gone.

'They wanted me to forget what happened yesterday,' Alice said, looking both angry and distressed. 'The bastards. Obviously seeing you out here drove all thoughts of reconciliation from their minds.'

'Are you going to make any sort of complaint against Ira?'

'I know I should. I'd be urging anyone else to do so. But, thanks to you, he didn't actually do anything. And some people would only accuse me and say it was my fault for the way I act. It'll cause more problems than it's worth.' Alice paused then, Wallace's words obviously having worried her, went on in a rush, 'Oh, Forbes, they won't carry out their threat will they? They won't get Billy taken away from me?'

'How can they? Who will the town believe? You, who they've known for a long time, or Wallace, who hasn't exactly endeared himself to anyone since his arrival? Everyone knows you're a good mother. And anyway how can they accuse you of misbehaving when you're sleeping in the house and I'm sleeping in the barn?'

'I suppose you're right.' Alice took a deep breath and immediately returned to her usual self, saying, 'Oh by the way, Forbes, there's plenty of hot water left. Why don't you use it to have a bath? There's a tin bath in the shed. You can take that into the kitchen.'

'Ma'am I work here, you don't own me.'

Alice went on as if he hadn't spoken. 'And if you wash your hair I'll cut it into a more decent length for you.'

'Yes ma'am.' Gritting his teeth, Forbes walked away, muttering something very impolite about women under his breath.

Alice pretended not to hear, instead she

160

went back inside to get a pair of scissors.

'That's a situation that needs to be kept an eye on,' Wallace said to Hamilton as they rode away. 'Oh I'm quite sure nothing improper is going on but others might be persuaded that it is. Maybe that's something we can use to our advantage.'

'Yes, sir.' Hamilton felt he'd be willing to do, or say, anything to anyone to get his own back on Forbes. He didn't like being bested in any kind of fight, and he felt that Forbes had done just that. Not only had he stopped Ira having his way with Mrs Munroe, but now he was probably doing just that himself. No, Hamilton was unhappy and the unhappier he was the meaner he became.

Marshal Patterson sat at his desk, head in his hands, wondering, not for the first time, what to do. What had happened to Paul Broome was bad enough, what had happened to Casey Chapman was a disgrace. And the assault had taken place in town. The fact that Hamilton and the others lived out of town was no excuse for him not to do something about it.

Now Chapman was threatening to press charges and several of the citizens, led by Laura Reynolds' father, were urging him to act.

And Patterson wanted to act himself. He didn't like what was going on any more than anyone else. And he certainly didn't want to have to arrest the Broomes or help with any trial against them. So far he hadn't contacted the law in Laramie but doubtless Richard Wallace would be urging him to do so soon. Unless...

Maybe what they'd done to Chapman was providential after all.

A trade off.

If Chapman agreed. The Marshal got to his feet and picked up his hat. He'd go see Casey, have a talk with him.

Laura sat on the bed watching as Paul, a large bruise discolouring his cheek, stood in front of the mirror, combing his hair. He'd just finished dressing.

'Are you sure you're all right to go? I

wish you'd stay a while longer and rest up some more.'

Paul looked at her reflection in the glass. 'I can't, sweetheart. I must go back home in case there's any more trouble with Hamilton. Pa might need help.'

That was what Laura was afraid of.

'You know that awful man, Forbes, has left the Rocking W and is now out at Mrs Munroe's? How can she have him there with her? I'd be so scared if it was me.'

'I don't understand it either. But I guess she must have her reasons. Still even if she trusts him, I don't. Next time I see him what happens might be a different story.' And deliberately Paul reached down for his cartridge belt which he'd laid on a chair.

Laura had been born and raised on the frontier where guns were a way of life. If Paul didn't carry a gun then he risked being shot down without the chance to defend himself. For someone like Ira Hamilton, and maybe even Forbes, wouldn't care if his victim was unarmed.

Downstairs the cafe door banged and

Laura went over to the window. Her father was hurrying down the road towards the barber's. 'Pa's gone out. He'll be gone for quite a while.' Smiling she turned back to Paul. 'You don't really have to go just yet, do you?'

Paul grinned. Maybe he wasn't in that much of a hurry after all. He went over to the girl taking her into his arms.

'Be assured, Marshal, I won't allow my men to act in such a way again.' Richard Wallace smiled in his most sincere manner, hands resting on the desk in front of him. 'I was quite appalled when I heard about poor Mr Chapman. It was contrary to my orders I can assure you.'

'That's all very well,' Patterson said. 'But they ought to be arrested for violence and destruction of property.'

'Chapman won't press charges. And if he does I shall offer to pay him for the damage caused. He'll be satisfied with the money.'

Patterson was astonished at the arrogance of the man. Clearly Wallace thought of everything in the light of money and believed everyone else did so as well.

'I need my men for the Spring round up,' he went on. 'Surely you can see that? If I give my word they won't cause any more trouble that will be enough.'

'Not necessarily. However, I think Mr Chapman can be persuaded not to press charges...'

'Ah!'

'...so long as you agree to drop the charges against the Broomes.'

For a moment Wallace looked at the lawman as if he couldn't believe, or understand, what he'd said. 'But I'm in the right!' he stated at last.

'And so is Mr Chapman. Any jury, either here in Fairmont or in Laramie, will find your men guilty. The evidence against them is overwhelming, whereas that against the Broomes, given their unblemished past record, is doubtful. They might not be convicted. Iffen I were you, Mr Wallace, I'd do as I suggest. Be best all round, wouldn't you say?'

# FOURTEEN

Forbes and Alice rode out several times to see where her cattle were. Billy always came along, riding on the horse in front of his mother and, because it meant being out most of the day, they took along sandwiches and home made lemonade. Naturally Alice didn't have as much land or as many cattle as Richard Wallace but to Forbes' inexperienced eyes, the cattle appeared fat and healthy and amongst them were numerous unbranded calves. He only hoped they weren't calves rustled from the Rocking W and wisely kept quiet on the subject.

'What are you going to do when round up time comes?' Forbes asked. He and Alice sat on the edge of a meadow eating the meal she'd prepared, while Billy went off exploring amongst the flowers and undergrowth. 'Hire more men?'

Alice shook her head. 'I only wish I could, but I could never afford them. The Broomes have promised to help. We'll probably put all our cattle together. It's not ideal but I don't see what else I can do. I can't gather up the cattle on my own, nor could I drive them to market. Mr Broome won't cheat me. Mr Forbes, will you stay and help take the cattle to the railhead?'

Forbes hesitated, not liking to give a commitment he might not be able to fulfil.

'I'd understand if you don't want to,' Alice said.

'It's not that I don't want to,' Forbes said, lying back on the grass. 'It's just that I ain't used to all this work.'

'I see.' Alice then added craftily. 'But if you stay on until I've sold my cattle I'll be able to pay you at least something for all you've done.'

'Mebbe then,' Forbes said and grinned at her. She gave him a smile back; but it was only a small one, as if she hadn't smiled in a long while and had almost forgotten how.

'Now we'd better go back, there's a lot to do.'

'Oh, Mrs Munroe, why don't you lighten up for once? It's a lovely day, Billy is enjoying himself, so am I. Why don't you? Just for a while.'

Alice looked uncertain. Then she said, 'All right.' But Forbes felt she wasn't happy as she sat, stiff backed, her arms wrapped round her drawn up knees.

'Mrs Munroe, do you think Richard Wallace really believes you're all rustlers? Or is he using it as an excuse?'

Alice frowned. 'I don't know. He doesn't seem to know a lot about ranching and he's had to depend very much on Ira Hamilton since he came here.'

'Perhaps if he'd had someone other than Hamilton as his foreman things might have been different.'

'Maybe but I doubt it. Even Wallace must know the sort of man Hamilton is yet he employs him. Why, if he doesn't mean to use him and his gun? I think that Wallace is a greedy young man who, even if the rustling wasn't his idea, has found it very convenient to believe Hamilton. He's a fool. With all his land he could have been a success without wanting more. I also believe that Hamilton himself drove those cows onto the Broomes' land and left the running iron behind.'

'He could have done,' Forbes admitted. 'He'd have had the time.'

'You had nothing to do with that?'

'No ma'am, truly. I've been a fool and believed what Wallace and Hamilton told me and did what they told me to do. Mostly for the money. But I didn't do anything wrong. And I'm sorry for it all. Do you believe me?' Forbes hoped she did.

'Yes, Mr Forbes, I do.'

To his own considerable surprise, Forbes found himself slipping into the work of the ranch, if not eagerly, then at least willingly. No doubt about it, Alice Munroe was a hard taskmaster. It was always do this or do that. There was never a minute to himself. And he wasn't altogether sure about taking orders from a woman. Yet

Forbes felt he couldn't complain because however hard she worked him, then she was willing to do exactly the same.

And more. For as well as the outdoors work—mending fences, cutting wood, looking after the garden—she had the cooking and work in the house to do as well. And she did it well, although her language left a lot to be desired.

'I'm surprised at how well you manage it all,' Forbes said one morning, after he'd been there just over a week.

'Never expected a woman could do such manly things, eh?' Alice laughed, bitterly.

'It was meant to be a compliment.' Forbes wondered why she always had to be so prickly.

'I know. Me doing all this was a matter of necessity. When my husband...died, I had to learn what to do or go under. I had no choice. But it's not been easy.'

The two of them went out of the door, into the early morning sunshine.

'You've done wonders with the vegetable garden, Mrs Munroe.'

Alice had spent much of her time clearing

170

the weeds, digging up rotting vegetables and planting new seeds. Already small green shoots were pushing their way up through the earth to the surface.

'I like seeing things grow. I always have. And vegetables are both good to eat and cheap to grow.'

They paused to watch Billy struggling up the slope from the river, carrying a bucket of water. Full up when he started it was now less than half full where he'd spilled most of it.

Alice went to help but Forbes stopped her. 'He needs to do things for himself. To learn and grow up.'

'I sometimes feel he's had to grow up too soon. He's only six.'

'I know, but that's the way it is sometimes.'

'You think I mother him too much?'

'No, he's a good kid. You've done well by him. But it won't do him any good to remain a boy when he needs to be a man.'

Billy spent most of his time with Forbes. Forbes wasn't sure what to make of the boy, and usually only spoke to him to give him orders. And the boy rarely spoke to him, except to say 'Yes, Mr Forbes' or 'No, Mr Forbes'. But slowly, almost unrealized by either of them, their uneasiness with each other got better. They got used to one another. And the boy was certainly a willing worker, fetching and carrying and doing whatever he could to help.

'Billy misses his father and a man's influence. He doesn't really trust anyone any more. I've done my best but I do wonder at times whether it's good for him to be out here with just me, his mother, for company. Is it enough?'

Forbes shrugged. 'It's all there is.'

He started across the yard. Before he was halfway to the corral where he was mending the fence, he felt the boy's presence, like a shadow, walking by him. Forbes' arm was swinging by his side and much to his surprise Billy's hand slipped into his. His first reaction was to pull away—goddammit he didn't like kids—but he knew it was important that he didn't. Instead he held the boy's hand tightly and, goddammit, it suddenly felt good.

Watching from the house, Alice felt tears prick her eyes. It was the first time in a long while that Billy had trusted anyone enough to make the first move to touch them. She turned away and went inside so that Forbes wouldn't see what he might consider weakness on her part. Please, she thought, don't let anything go wrong, not now.

That night after supper, Alice said, 'Forbes, don't go yet.'

'Ma'am?'

'It's a lovely evening.' It was one of the first really warm evenings of the year. 'Sit outside with me for a while.'

'Well...I...don't know.'

'Please. Have a drink with me. You deserve it.'

Forbes was pleasantly surprised that Alice thought he deserved something other than hard work and even more surprised that for once her idea of a drink wasn't the usual water or lemonade but whiskey! As she brought out a nearly full bottle and two glasses, he suddenly realized that he hadn't had a drink since his arrival at the ranch. If he'd known she had a bottle stashed somewhere it might well have been a different matter.

'Just one glass mind,' she said.

They sat in the old rockers outside the front door, facing the sunset, looking towards the river. Forbes was shocked all over again when she poured some whiskey out for herself as well and sipped at it as if she was quite used to it. He'd been sure she'd have lemonade.

They drank slowly, not even bothering to make small talk, but somehow the silence between them wasn't awkward. And Forbes was sorry when the whiskey was finished, not because he was desperate for more, which for once he wasn't, but because he had no excuse to stay longer.

'I'd better be going, ma'am, lots to do tomorrow.'

'Yes, all right. Goodnight, Forbes.'

'Goodnight, Mrs Munroe.'

# FIFTEEN

'Really, Alice, what the hell is he doing here?' Casey Chapman nodded angrily out of the open door towards where Forbes was busy chopping wood. As usual, Billy stood nearby helping him by stacking up the wood. 'Honestly, I couldn't believe it when I heard. I told everyone there had to be some mistake. That it was a rumour put about by Wallace...'

'So there are rumours concerning me and Forbes?'

'Of course there are!' Chapman exclaimed. 'What else did you expect? A widow living out here all on her own with a man, a stranger, who looks and behaves like a drunken gunhand, for company. Of course people are talking.'

'They have nothing to gossip about. Forbes works for me, he sleeps in the barn. They wouldn't say anything if I'd hired a couple of men from Fairmont.'

'That would have been different.'

'I don't see how. And what business is it of their's anyway? None of the town's good citizens rushed out here to help me around the ranch. Forbes was the only one willing to stay.'

'And why do you think that was?'

'Because he didn't realize what he was getting into at the Rocking W.'

'I never thought you a fool, Alice! You're being taken in by him.'

'No, I'm not. He's worked well since he's been here, even though he knows I can't pay him, not yet anyway. He's behaved in the most proper way. And Billy likes him. Oh, Casey, it's good to have a man about the place again.'

Chapman sighed. That was the trouble. Alice did have a man to help her again and he was jealous. 'All right, I understand. But be careful and be warned. You might not get such a favourable reaction when next you're in Fairmont.'

'If people want to believe the worst of me then that's up to them. I haven't got

time to worry, I've got a ranch to run.'
Alice spoke more bravely than she felt. The
opinion of at least some of her friends was
important to her and she didn't want to
become any more of an outcast than she
already was. But what was the alternative?
There was no way she could send Forbes
away. 'Are you ready?'

'Yes, sure.'

The real reason for Chapman's visit to
the ranch was for him to accompany Alice
to a meeting of the ranchers. Since the
beating up of both Paul Broome and
himself and the destruction of his office,
and with feelings running high, Wallace
and his men had been quiet. That didn't
mean they would remain so. Wallace was
still fuming over having to give in to
Patterson's blackmail and not have the
Broomes stand trial. And the Spring
round-up and the branding of the new
born calves happening any day now, would
make an ideal time for the unscrupulous
rancher to attack his neighbours.

So Alice had called a meeting and
invited Chapman along so that he could

report on it in his paper.

'Not that the poor old *Enquirer* is up to much these days,' Chapman told Alice as she put on her jacket and old hat. 'Just a handwritten broadsheet that I copy out and pin up in places around town for people to read.'

'So long as they read it.' Alice looked anxiously at Chapman. He still had a black eye but his other cuts and bruises had almost gone. He'd also gotten some new spectacles. 'How are repairs going?'

'Slowly. I don't think the printing press can be repaired. I shall have to buy a new one and that takes money I don't have right now. Perhaps it is time for me to move on.' Chapman looked hopefully at Alice, wondering if she would ask him to stay. She said nothing. 'But I don't want Wallace to think he's frightened me into running.'

'I'm sure no one would think any of the worse of you if you did leave but we'd all miss reading the truth.'

Outside Forbes had finished chopping wood. He knew only too well that

Chapman was discussing him with Alice and he hoped that he wouldn't say enough to make her send him on his way. Alice would be fair but if it came to a choice between him or Billy, he knew what would happen. The buckboard was ready and now seeing Alice and Chapman coming out of the house, Forbes lifted Billy up into the front seat and went to get his own horse.

'He's not coming with us, is he?' Chapman spoke in dismay.

'Yes, I asked him to.'

'Was that wise?'

'I thought it might be if Wallace or Hamilton had gotten to hear about this meeting and wanted to stop us reaching it.'

'I daresay you're right. But I'm not sure how the others will react after what Forbes did to young Paul.'

The meeting was to be held at the Broomes' ranchhouse. Most of those who were going to take part were already there when Forbes, Alice and Chapman arrived. Reaction to Forbes was mixed. Some people seemed scared as if thinking he was going to start shooting at them; others, remembering his drunken exploits in town, were disgusted, while the majority were angry, wondering if Alice had taken leave of her senses in bringing him along.

As Forbes helped Alice and Billy down from the buckboard, Broome hurried up and planted himself in front of Forbes, hands on hips, while Paul stood nearby looking as if he itched to start a shooting match. 'After all you've done, you've got one helluva nerve to come here,' he said. 'It was lucky Paul wasn't worse hurt. Alice, he really ain't welcome.'

'He's with me,' Alice said crossly. 'He goes, I go.' She turned to Forbes. 'I'm sorry about this. I thought they'd understand or at least give me a chance to explain.'

'It's all right.' At times Forbes had received far frostier receptions than this. All the same he wasn't really sure why he'd come. All this trouble was nothing to do with him. He was just an unpaid hired hand. He didn't need this sort of aggravation. He hadn't even been able to have a drink to bolster his courage to meet the hostility of these people. But their hostility was understandable. No one was to know that he'd been fooled by Richard Wallace and that he liked the rancher's actions no more than they did. He had done nothing to make anyone but Alice think he could be trusted. 'If they want me to go, I will.'

'No,' Broome shook his head. He knew Alice better than Forbes did and realized well enough that she would carry out her threat to leave with him. Alice might only be a woman but she was needed in the fight against Richard Wallace. 'You can stay. But don't cause any trouble. Come on, Alice, we'll all discuss what we're going to do and then there's food and drink laid on.'

Forbes stood a little way off as Broome led Alice over to where the rest were gathering out by the corral. They went to the front and gradually the men, women and children quietened and turned expectant faces towards them.

Paul brushed by Forbes. 'You might have fooled Mrs Munroe, you might have got on Pa's right side, but you ain't fooling me.'

'Look, I don't want any trouble with you. I'm sorry for what happened.'

'Oh, sure. I don't trust you, Mr Forbes, not one bit. I'll be keeping an eye on you.'

'That's up to you but seems to me we've got to work with one another so we might as well try to get along.' From the scowl Paul gave him, Forbes felt his attempt at reconciliation had fallen on stony ground.

'Thanks for coming,' Broome opened the meeting. 'I know how busy you all are, especially at this time of the year, but it's important to get together and see what we're going to do about the continuing threat of Wallace and his Rocking W. His holdings are growing day by day and soon he'll be all round us.'

'He ain't approached us yet,' said a bearded rancher sitting at the front. 'Are you sure the reason you're so worried ain't because of the notice put on your door and because of what happened to your boy?'

'Of course I'm concerned about myself

but I've also been concerned about those of my neighbours who've been forced to sell out to Wallace.'

'If we don't all stand together what's happening to those near to Wallace today could happen to those further away tomorrow,' Alice reminded them.

There were several mutters of agreement but also some shakes of heads from others.

'I dunno,' the bearded man said. 'Mr Wallace has always acted decent with us.'

'Sure he has. Just like he was all right to Casey and to Paul. You all know what happened to them.'

'Is going around beating up innocent men and destroying their property the actions of an honest man?' Broome added.

'It wasn't him who did it, it was his men. We all know who was responsible.'

All eyes were turned towards Forbes who felt most uncomfortable at the unfriendly scrutiny. There were a few mutters of drunk and scum.

A woman called out: 'Really, Mrs Munroe, you're a fine one to lecture us when you've got that creature living out at your ranch with you.'

Alice went red. Scared she would lose her temper and alienate them further by giving them a tongue lashing, with some bad language to go along with it, Broome touched her arm, and quickly said,

'What happened was condoned by Wallace. Has he given any of his men the sack, offered any sort of apology? No, of course not. Don't be fooled by him. You all know what happened to Mrs Munroe's husband. It could happen to any of you.'

There was a stirring at this, and people refused to look at one another.

'Wallace is a man who wants his own way and will stop at nothing to get it.'

'OK, supposing you're right, what can we do about it? We all know on whose side the law is going to be.'

'We're not talking about doing anything against the law, or even asking the law for help,' Alice said. 'What we are talking about is being careful. We must all help one another, watch each other's backs. Get together during round up and ride patrol on one another's herds. Or else risk the loss of them.'

There was a lot of further muttering at this, most of it against what Alice had said. To get together in such a manner maybe meant the loss of business or profits. That wasn't natural, especially to a small rancher trying to scrape a living from a sometimes harsh land. Money meant the difference between survival or going under.

Forbes could see the way it was going. Most of the men agreed with Broome and Alice, until it came to their pockets, while most of their wives were scared and would leave if only there was somewhere to go to. There would be little or no agreement reached here, until others besides the Broomes and Alice were threatened. If Wallace didn't win by one method he could always use the old way of 'divide and conquer'. And Forbes knew his presence wasn't helping matters. Most of the women were disgusted at Alice for having him at the ranch, quite prepared to believe that they were sleeping together. Whatever had happened in the past, whatever she had done for them, they were now using him as an excuse to influence their husbands against her and do whatever Wallace wanted.

He shook his head and noticed Casey Chapman standing near to him. 'They should do as Mrs Munroe wants and stick together. That's the only way of defeating someone like Wallace.'

Chapman shot a look at him that had no friendliness in it. 'What do you know? Anyway what business is it of yours? You'll be moving on soon. If you really feel that way why don't you get up there and voice your opinions?'

Forbes said nothing. He was no good at speaking before an audience. If he stood up there he'd only make more of a fool of himself than they already thought him.

The meeting finished without reaching any sort of conclusion. With something like relief that that was over and done with, everyone made their way to where the food and drink was laid out on gingham covered tables set out in the shade of the barn.

'I really don't feel like staying and eating with them,' Alice said crossly.

'If you don't you risk upsetting them more,' Forbes pointed out. 'Some of 'em are still on your side. The others will be too once Wallace gets round to them.'

'By then it might be too late.'

'You mustn't give up. That's not like you.'

'Come and eat with us, Mrs Munroe,' Paul urged. 'Please. Ma has put out a special spread.'

Not sure if he was invited or not, Forbes followed Alice over to the tables and although no one spoke to him neither did they make any objection to his presence. Not for the first time he wondered why he stayed. Goddammit he could be back with Sallee and Ben Cook—people who liked him. Forbes didn't like being unpopular.

In the hills above the ranch, Ira Hamilton lay on his stomach hidden amongst some rocks, watching the gathering through Wallace's powerful binoculars. Although, naturally, he couldn't hear what was being said, he had no doubt what the speeches were about. Equally he couldn't know that no real decisions had been made.

As far as he was concerned, the sodbusters were getting together to make trouble for his boss. And they were being led not only by the Broomes, who should have known better, but by that trouble-making bitch, Alice Munroe, who couldn't keep quiet not even after all that had happened to her and her family.

And she still had that bastard, Forbes, with her. In fact, it looked like he'd got his feet well and truly under the table.

Wait till he reported this to Mr Wallace. Maybe this time his boss would agree that something had to be done and fast, especially after his failure with the Broomes.

Wallace might have several people he wanted to get his own back on; there were also quite a few names on Hamilton's list of those who needed teaching a lesson.

# SIXTEEN

On the drive home, Alice was quiet. She only spoke to invite Chapman in to share the evening meal.

'I'd like to try and get back to town before it gets dark,' he said. 'Don't take today to heart, Alice. You can't blame the others for looking after themselves. It's human nature.'

Alice smiled wearily. 'It's just so disappointing.'

Chapman took her hands in his for a moment. 'You know where I am if you want me.'

Supper was quiet as well. Billy was affected by his mother's mood and the pair of them hardly ate anything, pushing their food around their plates. Forbes was glad when the meal was over and he went outside, sitting on the rocker, waiting while Alice and Billy washed up and Alice put her son to bed. He waited for such a long time that he began to think Alice wasn't going to join him. He was deciding on whether or not to go back to the barn when the door opened and she came out.

Forbes gaped. He couldn't help himself. Alice had let her hair down and done something with it so that it fluffed out in a curly cloud around her shoulders. She'd also put on a dress—Forbes hadn't known she possessed such a thing. It was light blue and had short sleeves and a lacey low cut front so that her arms and neck were revealed, together with the first risings of her breasts.

He could hardly believe it was Alice. The hard riding, hard working Alice, who dressed like a man, swore like one and usually thought more of her cattle than of her own appearance. She was soft and feminine, pretty.

'There's no need to act so surprised,' she told him, as tartly as ever. 'I do sometimes like to look like a woman!' She sat down and poured them both out nearly full glasses of whiskey. 'You don't really think I want to go around wearing pants and knowing everyone is talking about me, do you? I saw your face the first time you saw me in trousers! Even someone like you thought I was the worst kind of slut. But I wear them because I have to. I couldn't do the work here any other way.'

Forbes ignored the 'someone like you' and said, 'I'm sorry. I know you're right.'

'I don't usually have time or inclination to bother but I felt like cheering myself up tonight.'

'It was worth the effort.'

'I suppose so. I'm down that's all.'

'Chapman's right. You can't force others to do what you want. You can only do what's right for yourself.'

'I know and I believe I am doing right. William, my husband, died for this place.' She glanced up at the grave on the rise and there were sudden tears in her eyes.

With an insight he didn't usually possess, Forbes saw Alice's vulnerability beneath the brashness and thought how brave she was. For not only was she having to do a man's job on the ranch, she also had to be a mother to a small boy, and fight off someone who wanted to take it all from her; and all on her own with no husband to help.

'We had so much, William, Billy and I,' she went on in a bleak tone. And began to cry.

Forbes sat awkwardly by her, not knowing what to do or say. The women he usually associated with weren't paid to cry in front of him. They were too busy wanting to see him on his way. After a while she snuffled into a handkerchief and wiped her eyes.

'I'm sorry, I never meant to do that.'

'Don't be silly, it's all right. Would it help to talk about it?'

Alice nodded wordlessly.

'How did your husband die?'

'Richard Wallace had him murdered!'

'Oh!' Forbes sat up straight with shock, although he wasn't sure why he should be so surprised.

'Nothing can be proved, of course. But my husband was the driving force behind getting the ranchers together to fight Wallace. He was succeeding too. Then one day William was late returning from a meeting in Fairmont. When he still wasn't back the next morning, Mr Broome and I went out looking for him. He'd been ambushed. Shot in the back and left to die.'

'It couldn't have been a robbery that went wrong?'

'That was the conclusion Marshal Patterson came to. I don't blame poor old Fred. Robbery with violence he could understand. But a murder like that was way beyond him. Naturally Wallace had a perfect alibi for the time it happened and no evidence was found against Ira Hamilton. But it was Hamilton who did it.' Alice's hands clenched into fists in her lap. 'And if Wallace didn't put him up to it he certainly knew afterwards and did nothing about it. The day after I buried William the bastard came round offering support and sympathy and a price on the ranch.' Her eyes darkened. 'If I'd had my gun with me I'd have shot the sonofabitch there and then and taken the consequences.'

'And since your husband's death the ranchers have been falling away in their support?'

'Most of them, yes. Or else they've sold up. Now it's really only me and the Broomes that are left so close to Wallace. We're standing in his way. I don't really know how much longer I can hold out. I suppose I can't blame the others. If what happened to William had happened to someone else's husband I'm sure I'd have been urging him to leave.'

'I doubt that.'

'There are times when I'm so scared all I want to do is run away.'

'But you don't. I think you're very brave.'

'Thank you.'

For a moment there was silence. Forbes looked at Alice. She looked back at him. Their eyes held and locked together. Forbes found himself going red like an innocent schoolboy. His heart was pounding. He suddenly longed to take her in his arms and kiss her. How could he? She was a lady, he was a saddlebum. She'd turn him away.

'I'd better go,' he said in a hoarse voice and stood up so abruptly he almost knocked his chair over.

Alice stood as well. 'Don't go.'

And almost without conscious thought, Forbes had his arms round Alice and was pulling her close. She didn't resist and his lips came down on hers. He felt her cling to him.

Christ! What was he doing?

With an effort he pushed her away. 'Mrs Munroe I...I'm sorry...I don't know what came over me.'

'Please Forbes,' she said, 'don't leave me tonight.'

'Do you really mean that?'

'Yes.'

And Forbes picked her up in his arms and carried her into the house, kicking the door shut behind him.

A long time later as they lay together in Alice's bed, the pale light from a full moon streaking across the room, Alice lifted her head slightly to stare up at him.

'In the circumstances I can hardly continue to call you Forbes. What's your Christian name?'

'It's Elliott, ma'am.'

Alice laughed. 'And it's not appropriate for you to call me ma'am or Mrs Munroe. Elliott is a nice name. Why don't you use it more often?'

'Oh I don't know, ma'am...Alice...it just seems that everyone calls me Forbes. I'm used to it.'

Forbes looked at her as she smiled gently. He couldn't believe he was here with her in her bed. He couldn't believe how making love to her had been so much better than making love to a prostitute. It had been different in a way he had difficulty in understanding. It had made him feel good, yet vulnerable too, as if he was scared he'd hurt her or let her down. And in the end she'd made him feel comfortable, as if at last he was home. His earlier doubts vanished. He now knew exactly why he stayed.

'How did you get to be the sort of

person you are? I mean this last week or so you've been helpful and kind and worked hard. Billy looks up to you which believe me isn't an easy thing to make him do. Yet when I first saw you you were a drunk and looked quite capable of being the man Wallace obviously thought you were. Which one is the real you?'

'I don't know, Alice,' Forbes thought hard. 'I guess I just drifted into becoming what I am...was. And no one would give me the chance to change. Or rather if I'm honest I didn't give myself that chance. I told myself I liked what I was doing. Wait, I'll show you something.'

He left the warm bed and Alice's soft embrace and went over to where he'd thrown his clothes. From a jacket pocket he pulled out a small leather wallet which he took back to the bed. When he opened it, Alice could just make out the photographs of two very young men, although she couldn't see their features.

'That's me and my younger brother, Joel. It was taken before the war.' Forbes could still clearly remember the day they had posed so proudly for the itinerant photographer who came to the village and set up his camera in the schoolhouse. How happy his parents had been. Jesus, what would they think now? 'I was a grave disappointment to my pa when I wouldn't join the Confederate States Army and fight for what he thought was my country, its freedom and future. Joel was the one who went away to fight. Pa was so proud and pleased that day Joel came home in his grey uniform, especially as he hadn't told anyone he was enlisting.'

'What happened to your brother?'

'Oh he was killed, shot down by some Yank, in some minor skirmish no one, except those involved, ever heard of. Poor pa couldn't even say Joel'd been killed in a major battle like Gettysburg. He was sixteen.'

'I'm sorry'

'It's a long time ago now. It just seems such a waste of all my parents' hopes for us both. Poor Joel dead and me nothing but a no good ruffian. Christ, Alice, I don't even know if my folks are still alive.'

'Don't worry, not now.' Alice pulled Forbes down in the sheltering comfort of her arms. 'You're a good man, Elliott. I love you.'

## SEVENTEEN

The following morning, Alice knew she should never have added the words 'I love you' to Forbes. It had been a dreadful mistake, only making him think that she meant to try and tie him down at the ranch; that maybe going to bed with him had been some way of tricking him into a commitment he wasn't ready for.

He had been remote with her all morning, hardly speaking, not looking her in the eye. His mind elsewhere.

And here was she, like a fool, having fallen for a no good idiot. For she had spoken the truth. She did love Elliott Forbes.

She thought she'd gotten used to being

alone and then he'd come into her life and she'd realized how lonely she had actually felt. With him around she was lonely no longer. She'd liked sitting outside with him in the evening, liked watching him at work, liked the way he and Billy had become friends. And now he was going away and she'd be on her own again.

Oh, damn him and damn all men!

Alice was right. Forbes was going to move on. The previous night had been something special, something he'd never forget, but of which he was now ashamed. Dammit Alice—Mrs Munroe—was a respectable woman, and only recently a widow. Worse, being respectable, would she expect him to marry her?

Marriage! Responsibilities! All his life, Forbes had fled from such things. He couldn't face up to them now. He wasn't ready. And while a small part of his mind said that if at thirty-five he wasn't ready then he was never likely to be—and that if he passed up the chance of staying with Alice and making a good home with her, he'd regret it all his life—the rest of him said get the hell out of there and go back to drinking, gambling and whoring. It wasn't fair to expect anything else of him.

He couldn't bring himself to even try to explain this to Alice or to say goodbye to her. He didn't want to see any more of the hurt in her eyes that had been there over breakfast. He'd leave and after a short while both she and Billy would forget all about him.

And surely Forbes would be able to forget all about them as well.

Feeling like a heel and hating himself, Forbes hastily got his saddlebags together, and went to the corral where his horse was. Billy was in the garden, doing some weeding. The boy looked up, stared at him for a moment, and then looked down again, carefully taking no more notice of him. Forbes saddled and bridled his horse, mounted and started back across the yard, towards the rise and the road to town.

He was halfway across the yard when he heard the door of the house open. From out of the corner of his eye he could see Alice standing there. But she made no move towards him and he made no move towards her either.

He was almost at the grave of William Munroe when in the distance he heard the bellowing of frightened cattle, yells and the occasional shot. And there stampeding towards the house, or rather being driven by three riders, were some fifty head of cattle.

Above their noise he heard Alice scream.

Christ! Billy!

Frantically, Forbes turned his horse's head and galloped back down the hill. 'Get inside!' he yelled at Alice, who was running towards her son. She hesitated a moment. 'Get in the house!' Flinging himself off the horse he raced towards Billy, picking him up in his arms and running for the barn. Halfway there the boy wriggled out of Forbes' desperate arms. 'Come here!'

'Ma! Ma!' Billy called.

'Billy! Quick!'

Forbes never saw if he made it in time. The cattle were almost on him. He had no choice but to run for the safety of the barn and dive through the entrance just as the first cattle hit the yard. 'Jesus Christ!' he moaned out loud as he hit the ground with a heavy thump. He lay there, heart pounding as the earth shook and bulky bodies hit the side of the barn. 'Please, let the walls hold,' he thought and scrambled to the doorway where he could do nothing but crouch watching the frightened, maddened animals.

Some of the cattle crashed through the corral, the fence breaking beneath the weight of the pushing, shoving bodies. After milling round they crashed through the other side, taking Forbes' horse with them. Even more bumped into the side of the barn and they all joined together to pound Alice's lovingly cared for vegetable garden into the ground.

As they approached the house, the men—Forbes recognized Hamilton, Del and Burt—fired their guns at walls and windows, shattering the glass. They were whooping with excitement. Then the cattle were making for the river. Driven across, the water churned into froth, they came to a slow, bewildered halt in the meadow while the three men rode away still firing their guns in the air.

Hardly able to see for the lingering dust, Forbes ran towards the house. Please let Alice be all right, please, he whispered, and Billy too. At least the boy must have made it inside for there was no sign of a small body in the yard.

He crashed through the door and in one glance took in the glass on the floor, the smashed crockery and in the middle of the room Alice crouching on her knees, Billy in her arms.

'Alice?'

She raised a ravished face towards him. 'It's Billy, he's been shot!'

'Oh God.' Forbes got on his knees beside them and slowly released the boy from his mother's panic stricken grasp. The relief he felt when he saw that Billy was still breathing was so great it left him shaking. There was blood spreading on the boy's trousers, which quickly Forbes ripped away. 'It's all right,' he said to Alice. 'The wound isn't bad.'

'You're just saying that!' she accused hysterically.

'No, I wouldn't do that. Look there isn't even a bullet hole, just a bad graze. Get some water and a cloth and bandage it up and he'll be all right.'

'They could have killed him.'

A grim look on his face, Forbes helped Alice patch up her son. Then he left her to put him in his bed and went outside. When the door opened and Alice came out to join him, he was standing, hands in his pockets, staring round at the destruction left in the stampede's wake.

'Maybe it ain't as bad as it looks. Maybe it can be repaired.' Forbes knew he was lying.

'No, it's useless.' Alice went over to what remained of her vegetable garden. She paused to bend down and touch a shoot as if she could save it. When she stood up she was sobbing bitterly and blindly she walked back into Forbes' sheltering grasp. 'I can't fight any longer. It's not worth it any more. I could have lost Billy. I've lost all this. I'm giving up and going.'

To go or stay? To leave Alice or stay and take on the battle? To let the bastards at the Rocking W get away with shooting a child or not? In the end Forbes knew there really wasn't any choice. 'No,' he said.

'What do you mean, no?' Alice raised her head to look at him. 'It's nothing to do with you. You were all set to leave.'

'Yeah and now I'm staying.'

'I don't care about the ranch, not any more. Wallace can have it. I saw my own child get shot. You don't know what that means.'

'No, I don't. But I love Billy too. I love you. It's why I have to do something. Wallace and his thugs can't be allowed to get away with this. Hamilton doesn't care who he hurts and neither does Wallace.' He took her hands. 'Alice, all my life I've run away from things. I ran away from the War. I didn't want to be involved. I've been doing the same ever since. I was going to run away from you. But life ain't always that easy. And this is one time I ain't going to quit. It's time I faced up to my responsibilities and made a stand. For you, for Billy and for myself.'

'Oh, Forbes, you don't have to.'

'Yeah, I do.'

'I don't want you to.'

'It's not what you want. It's what I want. I love you, Alice, I won't see you hurt any more.'

Alice could see it was no use arguing. Forbes' mind was made up. 'What are you going to do?'

'Take the fight to them. See how they like it.'

'Then I'm coming with you.'

'No. You've got to stop here with Billy. He needs you.'

'But even though you're a gunfighter, you can't handle all four of them.'

Forbes laughed. 'A gunfighter? I ain't sure where you figured that one out from.'

'Everyone knows you are.'

'Well contrary to what everyone might know, I ain't any sort of gunhand. I've never shot anyone in my life!'

'Oh, Forbes, you can't go, not all on your own. I don't want to lose you.'

Forbes took no notice. He was mad as

hell. He'd never felt like this before. He'd take them all on! He kissed her lightly. 'Don't worry, Alice. This is something that I have to do, no matter what. Just remember that I love you.'

Alice was desperate. The way Forbes had spoken made it sound as if he didn't expect to come back. All she could do was watch him ride away. What would she do if he was shot—killed? It would be all her fault and it would be even worse if she just let it happen. She had to do something.

Quickly she hitched up the horse to the buckboard and went into Billy. The boy was awake now, frightened and upset. As she took him in her arms, kissing his face, and stroking his hair, telling him it was all right, he said tearfully,

'Where's Mr Forbes? Is he going away?'

'No.' Alice kissed her son again and lifted him up into her arms. 'He'll be back. Now, sweetheart, you've got to be very brave and we've got to go to the Broomes.'

'You won't leave me will you?'

'No, dearest.'

It was obvious that Ira Hamilton had been at the Broome ranch before they'd gone to Alice's. The place looked even more devastated—the corral completely smashed, the porch in front of the house broken and hanging by one pole, part of the barn gone. And a row of washing crushed in the dirt. The family came out to greet Alice and could hardly take in the fact that Billy had been shot.

'Bring him inside,' Norah fussed. She looked too shocked to cry and while George Broome carried the boy into the house, she and Alice clung to one another in mutual sympathy. 'Oh, Alice, this is dreadful. I'm so sorry.'

'Where's Forbes?' Broome asked.

'Elliott, er Mr Forbes, has gone after them.'

'Are you sure he ain't gone to join them again? Seen that that's the better side to be?' Paul asked, red faced with the fury he felt at what had happened.

Alice flushed. 'No, he's not like them.'

For a moment she smiled as she remembered the previous night. 'He's gone to fight the four of them. I'm fearful he'll be killed. Oh, Mr Broome, please we've got to help him. He's doing this for me. For us. He needn't have gone. Please, you can't just let him be shot down.' Alice was near to tears. Annoyed she blinked them back.

'I'll ride into town,' Broome decided. 'Bring help. No one will put up with Billy, a child, being shot. We'll sort this out once and for all. We should have done it a long time ago, thank God it ain't too late.'

Anxiously Alice watched as the man rode away. 'He'll never get back in time,' she said fretfully. 'Forbes could be dead by the time the posse gets to the Rocking W.'

'Don't worry, Mrs Munroe, I'll go and help Mr Forbes,' Paul said.

'Paul! You can't!' Norah screamed.

'I must, Ma. Mrs Munroe is right. It's our fight as well. If Mr Forbes really is willing to help us then we can't just stand by and do nothing in return.'

210

'What will Laura do if you're hurt?' Norah asked.

Alice put a hand on the young man's arm. 'You needn't do this.'

'If Mr Forbes has no choice, then neither do I.'

## EIGHTEEN

The Rocking W was quiet when Forbes approached it. A few prime horses grazed in the corral, some cattle dotted the nearby meadow. Smoke came from one of the chimneys of the house. That was all.

Forbes grinned. It looked as if Hamilton and the other two were still out, maybe stampeding other cattle across someone else's home; it didn't matter. He was ready for them all.

Pulling out his revolver, he urged his horse into a gallop and the peace of the afternoon was broken. He rode towards the house, firing as he did so. Several

211

shots hit the windows, sending showers of glass flying inwards over the carpets. See how Wallace liked that!

The rancher was in his study, going over his books, which he couldn't make much sense of. At the first shot, he leapt to his feet and then had to duck as the window shattered and he was in danger of being struck by flying glass. 'What the hell!' He looked up in time to see Forbes gallop by, firing again and again. 'My God!' Pausing only to grab up the rifle hanging on pegs over the fireplace, he ran for the door.

Breathing heavily, Forbes stopped in front of the house just as the door was flung open and Wallace came pounding out onto the porch. Forbes pointed his revolver directly at him. 'Hold it right there!'

Wallace slid to a halt. 'You crazy sonofabitch! What do you think you're up to?'

'Don't like it when it happens to you, do you? 'Bout time someone gave you a taste of your own medicine.'

Behind him the bunkhouse door was

thrust open and Del and Burt raced up the slope towards the confrontation. So those two were here after all, good!

'Tell 'em to throw down their weapons,' he ordered. 'Or I'll shoot you between the eyes.'

'Put your guns down!' Wallace called, believing Forbes would do as he threatened. He looked terrified and angry. The two cowboys slithered to an undecided halt. 'Do as he says.'

'You put your rifle down as well, Mr Wallace.'

'Do it,' Wallace said to his men, who showed a reluctance to obey his orders. 'What do you mean by this, Forbes? A taste of my own medicine, what are you talking about?'

'You know very well what I mean. Your men have been out stampeding your neighbours' herds, destroying your neighbours' property! Shooting at Mrs Munroe. It's a wonder no one was killed.'

'I don't believe you.' Wallace called down to Del and Burt. 'It's not true, is it?'

'You see,' Forbes said to the two cowboys, 'your boss ain't about to support you. He'll say that he didn't know anything about it. He'll see that you take all the blame.'

'There's nothing for anyone to take the blame for,' Wallace said angrily.

'Then why don't we all ride back to Mrs Munroe's place and see the damage they caused?'

'It ain't our fault if the cattle stampeded,' Del said sulkily.

'It is if you're driving 'em.'

'Oh, this is all nonsense,' Wallace said. 'You've done it now, Forbes. You've attacked me and my house. I'll have you arrested and thrown into jail.'

'I wouldn't be so sure about that.' Forbes smiled grimly. On his way here, in his first flush of anger, his intention had been to kill Wallace and Hamilton; now he knew he couldn't just shoot them down. Even if they were killers, he wasn't. 'I'm the one going to take you back to Fairmont and let the town take care of you.'

'Oh, they won't do anything to me.'

'Yes, they will, now. You see, during your men's raids no one was killed, no, but Billy Munroe was shot and wounded. I reckon you and your men won't be any too popular.'

'Oh, God,' Wallace whispered and went very white, while Del and Burt looked at one another in dismay.

'We didn't mean it, honestly,' Burt whined and both Wallace and Del told him to shut up.

Ira Hamilton peered out from the barn. It was that bastard, Forbes. He'd known all along that the saddlebum was worthless trash and now Wallace was finding that out the hard way. Hamilton didn't care about his boss's discomfiture; the sonofabitch should have listened to him. Even so, Forbes couldn't be allowed to get away with what he was doing. Forbes' lesson had arrived.

Hamilton scuttled back into the barn and quickly climbed up the ladder to the top. Carefully he walked to the opening from which the hay was loaded into the wagons. He raised his rifle. And fired.

The first shot missed Forbes by a whisker. The second shot would have taken his head off but Forbes was already hurling himself out of the saddle and the bullet only grazed him, leaving a painful furrow across his back. He fell to the ground and tried to grab for the rifle in the saddle scabbard. But his horse was leaping away from him and it took off leaving him with just his almost empty revolver.

He saw Richard Wallace picking up his gun and down the slope Del and Burt were reaching for the weapons they'd dropped. Everything everyone had ever said about his lack of sense was true. What a fool he'd been not to find out where Hamilton was before starting on this! Hamilton was the one to fear. Now it looked like he was going to suffer for his stupidity. Another bullet from Hamilton's gun set up a spout of dust at his feet. Obviously surrendering wasn't an option and he couldn't beat all four men.

But Wallace was nearest! And Wallace

was raising the rifle to fire at him as well.

Forbes rolled on his back and shot at the rancher. The bullet took him in the side and with a shriek of pain and fright Wallace collapsed. He dropped the rifle and hugged himself, rolling around in agony.

Forbes swung back to Del and Burt and pulled the trigger. Nothing happened. Sweat blinded his eyes. He'd never be able to reload in time.

Wallace's rifle!

Forbes scrambled to his feet and made a dash for the fallen rancher. Seeing him coming, Wallace tried to snatch up the weapon but Forbes raced up the steps to the porch and kicked it out of the way, diving towards it himself. Bullets from three guns followed him.

'Mind Mr Wallace you stupid fools!' Hamilton yelled from the barn.

So Hamilton was still loyal to his boss? Maybe Forbes could use that to his advantage. Grabbing hold of Wallace, he pulled him up in front of him, both of them in a crouch. The rancher cried out in pain.

'Quiet!' And Forbes was dragging the man into the house, kicking the door shut.

Wallace collapsed on the floor, bleeding all over his carpet. 'Help! Help!' he called out weakly.

From somewhere behind him, Forbes heard a door open. He swung round bringing up the rifle, seeing Wallace's two foreign servants dithering in the doorway. 'Don't! This ain't your fight.' And the servants agreed, wisely retreating.

Forbes ran into the dining room and began to fire the rifle through the shattered window, wondering how long he could hold out. The men out there could circle the house and easily overpower him. Even with Wallace as a hostage he doubted that would stop Hamilton for long.

Bullets from three guns slammed into the walls, smashed into the furniture behind him. Then a wild shot hit his shoulder knocking him backwards, off his feet. Crying out, he fought against the black of unconsciousness. It wouldn't be long now before Hamilton realized what had happened and would come after him. He was dead, for sure.

'Forbes! Forbes!'

From what seemed a long way away, Forbes heard his name being called. With an effort he used the rifle to raise himself to his knees and saw a rider galloping for the house. Whoever it was had to be friendly because Hamilton directed his fire at him.

Paul Broome reached Del and Burt and galloped straight through them. Del was knocked off his feet by the horse and Burt started to run away. Paul circled the man, ducking as Del shot at him. He fired his own gun. Del went down and stayed down. Paul cast a contemptuous glance at Burt who, having reached the bunkhouse, had kept on going.

That left Ira Hamilton.

'Watch out!' Forbes yelled a warning.

Hamilton had stepped slightly forward to aim at Paul. The boy was so near to him, the foreman couldn't miss.

Ignoring the pain in shoulder and back, Forbes, still on his knees, rested the rifle against the window sill and aimed, pulling the trigger. The recoil of the rifle against the wound made him gasp but even as he sank back, he had the satisfaction of seeing Ira Hamilton double up. The man dropped his rifle, took a shaky step forward and then fell out of the barn. His scream of terror was abruptly cut off as he landed with a thump.

And everything was suddenly queit.

'Forbes, are you all right?' Paul had crashed into the house and was bending over him.

'Ow! My shoulder! My back! Of course I ain't all right.' Paul helped him into a sitting position. 'Where did you come from?'

'Mrs Munroe asked for help.'

'I thought you didn't like me?'

'I ain't sure I do. But I've always liked and trusted Mrs Munroe and I decided she couldn't be all wrong about you. So I thought I'd better oblige. Looks like I got here just in time. Pa has gone to town to collect a posse. They should be here soon.'

But they wouldn't have got there in time. Forbes owed Paul his life.

'Help me up.' With Paul's support, Forbes went outside. Hamilton and Del were dead.

'And Burt's long gone,' Paul said with a grin. 'I reckon he'll run right into the posse.'

Inside the house, Richard Wallace was still slumped against the wall. He looked very pale and the side of his white shirt was red with blood.

'Well, was it worth it?' Forbes asked him.

'Sonofabitch.' He coughed. 'You'd better get me a doctor. I'm shot.'

'You ain't that badly hurt. Did you hear what Paul said? A posse will be here any moment. Iffen I was you when they arrive I'd make sure they knew I was packing up and leaving.'

Surprise came into Wallace's eyes. 'Leave? Why should I leave?'

The man's arrogance surprised Forbes

and it was with some pleasure that he said, 'Because, Mr Wallace, it's more than likely that after what happened to Billy the posse will come armed with hanging ropes.'

'I didn't shoot anyone.'

'You was responsible. You can't hide behind your money and your men any longer.'

'I can't go. I can't fail again. My father will never forgive me if I do.'

Forbes shrugged. 'You should have thought about that before.'

'Christ, Mr Wallace,' Paul said. 'If you don't take Mr Forbes' advice, I might shoot you myself.'

It wasn't long after that in the distance they saw the posse from Fairmont approach at a gallop, led by George Broome, Casey Chapman and the Marshal.

Forbes sat in a chair on the porch watching as they rode up to where Paul waited, ready to tell them what had happened. With the help of the servants, Paul had patched him up as best he could. Forbes knew that while both wounds hurt a lot, they weren't serious. He'd be over them in time to help Alice with the Spring round-up.

He smiled. He could just imagine her pacing up and down, fretting over what might be happening; probably cussing at the same time. And Billy too; was he missing him?

It was over now. The small ranchers of Fairmont could go back to the normal, settled lives they'd been living before Richard Wallace's arrival on the scene. Forbes wasted no time in feeling sorry for the young man, who had indeed failed yet again. It was his own fault. He'd had more of a chance than most people ever got to succeed and, wanting too much too quickly, hadn't taken it.

All Forbes wanted to do was leave the Rocking W and go back to where Alice waited for him.

He loved her and Billy. His place was with them, making a good future for them all.

This Large Print Book for the Partially sighted, who cannot read normal print, is published under the auspices of

**THE ULVERSCROFT FOUNDATION**